The Sound of Death

Toad was puffing on a cheroot. Freddie was spitting tobacco juice. Neither man was looking in Brad's direction when he drew his pistol and stepped in front of them. He pulled his rattles out with his left hand and shook them.

Both men stopped in their tracks.

"What the hell . . ." Toad said.

Then he heard the click of the Colt in Brad's hand as he cocked the trigger.

"Who in hell are you?" Toad demanded, jerking the cheroot from his mouth.

"They call me Sidewinder," Brad said and shook the rattles again.

He watched both men as the color drained from their faces . . .

SIDEWINDER

JORY SHERMAN

BERKLEY BOOKS, NEW YORK

THE BERKLEY PUBLISHING GROUP
Published by the Penguin Group
Penguin Group (USA) Inc.
375 Hudson Street, New York, New York 10014, USA
Penguin Group (Canada), 90 Eglinton Avenue East, Suite 700, Toronto, Ontario M4P 2Y3, Canada
(a division of Pearson Penguin Canada Inc.)
Penguin Books Ltd., 80 Strand, London WC2R 0RL, England
Penguin Group Ireland, 25 St. Stephen's Green, Dublin 2, Ireland (a division of Penguin Books Ltd.)
Penguin Group (Australia), 250 Camberwell Road, Camberwell, Victoria 3124, Australia
(a division of Pearson Australia Group Pty. Ltd.)
Penguin Books India Pvt. Ltd., 11 Community Centre, Panchsheel Park, New Delhi—110 017, India
Penguin Group (NZ), 67 Apollo Drive, Rosedale, North Shore 0632, New Zealand
(a division of Pearson New Zealand Ltd.)
Penguin Books (South Africa) (Pty.) Ltd., 24 Sturdee Avenue, Rosebank, Johannesburg 2196,
South Africa

Penguin Books Ltd., Registered Offices: 80 Strand, London WC2R 0RL, England

SIDEWINDER

A Berkley Book / published by arrangement with the author

PRINTING HISTORY
Berkley edition / December 2009

Copyright © 2009 by Jory Sherman.
Cover illustration by Bill Angresano.
Cover design by Lesley Worrell.
Interior text design by Laura K. Corless.

ISBN: 978-0-425-23148-7

BERKLEY®
Berkley Books are published by The Berkley Publishing Group,
a division of Penguin Group (USA) Inc.,
375 Hudson Street, New York, New York 10014.
BERKLEY® is a registered trademark of Penguin Group (USA) Inc.
The "B" design is a trademark of Penguin Group (USA) Inc.

PRINTED IN THE UNITED STATES OF AMERICA

10 9 8 7 6 5 4 3 2 1

For Grahame Hopkins,
the artist who awakened
the sleeping painter in me.

ONE

❧

The cattle were scattered amid the burned ruins of a cabin, with its stone chimney stark against the sky, its upper bricks crumbled into dust, and rubble at its base. The corrals were all jumbled wreckage, scrambled pine poles ripped from their moorings and scorched like the logs of the cabin.

Brad Storm, a tall, rugged man with flaxen hair, blue eyes as hard as sapphires, a square jaw, a soft crease dimpling the center of his chin, and the strong, supple hands of a wood-carver or a violinist, reined up his horse, a strawberry roan gelding with a splotchy white blaze on its forehead. The rider with him, his helper, Julio Aragon, halted his horse, a six-year-old pinto he called Chato. Julio had the high cheekbones of an Indian ancestor, the faint vermilion of his bloodlines coloring his cheeks, a bent nose that had once been straight. Coal black eyes glittered like polished agates in their sockets, and his black curly hair streamed down his neck and flared over his shoulders like downy oil.

"What is this place, Julio?" Brad asked.

A shadow passed across Julio's face, but it was not from any cloud or leafy tree branch. It was the shade of remembrance, and there was a wince in his features as the memory blossomed into life just beyond the flat bronze plate of his forehead.

"This was where Alberto Seguin once lived," Julio said, and there was a tinge of sadness in his voice. "Before you came here. He raised cattle. Big herd. Many head."

"What happened?" Brad asked.

Julio hung his head and shook it slowly from side to side. His hand on his saddle horn tightened until the veins stood out like worms under beige sand.

"The rustlers. Bad men from Oro City, I think. They stole all his cattle. Alberto fought them. They killed him, his wife, and two sons. They burned down his house and the corrals. The barn you can no longer see. It was only ashes, and they blew away in the wind."

"Damn. A shame. Anyone ever catch the rustlers?"

A steely look came into Julio's eyes and his jaw tightened until Brad could see the pulse in his left jawbone.

"The rustlers still ride. They still steal."

"Here? Where?"

"All over. No one catches them. No one ever catches them. They been stealing since before they called the territory Colorado and made it a state."

"Why?" Brad knew that Colorado had become a state only two years before, in 1876.

"There are many graves of those who tried to catch them, Brad."

"Maybe I better start guarding my cattle."

"You do not have enough yet to interest them. They look for the big herds. Five hundred to one thousand head, maybe."

Brad was just starting out as a cattle rancher. He had only two hundred head, plus a few yearlings. He had a breeding bull and a few brood cows. He planned on having many more. Beef was at a premium in the mining camps scattered throughout the Rockies.

A fresh breeze whiffled through the burned timbers of the house and set up a soft keening as if voices rose whispering from the dead. He felt a spider crawl up his spine and shook off the feeling.

"When your cows are already fat," Julio said, "and your herd is big, so the rustlers will come. They will come in the night and you will not see them."

"I'll be damned if they will, Julio. Everything I own is in those cows I have."

"That is of no import to the thieves."

"No, but hot lead will be."

"Ah, you are one man. They are many."

"I have you. At least I think I do."

"Two men against many." Julio crossed himself, and Brad heard him murmur, "Jesus, Mary, and Joseph," under his breath in Spanish.

"We'll see," Brad said. He looked over at the scattered cows. He began to count.

"We're one short," he said.

"Yes, the brindle cow. She is carrying a calf."

"You have a good eye."

"She was one of those that wandered off with these."

"She's probably in the timber."

"Maybe," Julio said, and there was the leaden weight of doubt in his voice. Cattle were herd animals, Brad knew, and it was unlikely the brindle cow had wandered out of sight and smell of the others.

Brad knew the cow was not in the timber, would not venture into that dark region alone. She should be with the other cattle, battling with them over the best graze. He knew her nature. He had studied her for nigh on to a year. She was big boned, wide hipped, with sturdy legs and plenty of muscle on her bones, the kind of cow that would produce sound calves that would grow into valuable beef cattle.

So, where was she?

"Gather 'em up, Julio, and run 'em back home. I'm going to look for the brindle."

"You no want me to help?"

"No, you go on. I'll track her down."

"Yes, boss," Julio said.

Brad frowned. He'd told Julio a hundred times not to call him "boss." He didn't want a title for himself, and the term implied a difference in social stations he didn't like. He thought of Julio as an equal, not as a man subservient to him. He waved a hand at Julio and turned his horse, craning his neck to the left in order to study the tracks on the ground.

It did not take Brad long to find the place where the brindle separated herself from the other cattle. She had wandered, nipping grass with her teeth, heading away from the other cows at an angle. It was when the tracks led him to a lush patch of grass near the edge of the timber that he saw the other tracks, and the sight of them sent an ice water shiver up his spine.

There was no mistaking the tracks of the brindle cow. She was bigger than the other yearlings that had strayed, and heavier. Her hooves had sunk deep into the moist earth around the grass. But, it was the other tracks that sent spiders crawling up his back.

A wolf track, still fresh, crisscrossed the cow tracks, and from its stride, Brad figured it was a timber wolf and would measure nine feet from tail tip to snout.

He turned to yell out his find to Julio, but he saw only the crown of the man's hat as he and the strays disappeared off the tabletop. Brad drew in a breath and listened to the soft sough of the wind in the pines and spruce and junipers. He was alone, and one of his cows was in trouble.

Big trouble.

He loosened his rifle in its boot and slapped the butt of his Colt .45. The Winchester was on half cock, with a shell in the chamber.

He let out his breath and began following the tracks. They led downward on an angle, away from the small mesa, and the ground was so uneven, rocky, and bramble-strewn that he could not see very far ahead. He leaned back against the cantle of his saddle as his horse descended down the steep slope, picking its way carefully over rough terrain.

The sky to the west was strewn with lavender clouds, their underbellies the soft pink of salmon. The sun was setting, and there was not much time if he was going to rescue that cantankerous cow and drive her back to his ranch. There was moisture in the wolf's tracks, but the cow's hoof marks were already turning dry.

In the distance, a red-tailed hawk sailed over the pine tops, its head turning from side to side as it hunted prey.

The loaves of clouds to the west began turning to ash, while the skyline glowed like a blacksmith's forge. When the sun set, he knew, the air would turn freezing cold and the green mountains would turn into huge lumps of lampblack.

TWO

❧

Brad awoke the following morning, determined to find the missing cow. By noon he hadn't had any luck. Above him, jays flitted through the trees like scraps of blue sky fluttering through the green branches of the pines. They were almost silent, but Brad was aware of them, his senses honed to a fine edge. A man alone in the wild had to be a part of it, or its wildness could devour him. There were cougars and bears in that part of the country, not to mention rattlesnakes and humans less attuned to nature than he was, nimrod hunters who shot at sounds without seeing the animal itself.

He gave his horse its head as it picked its way downslope, Brad's gaze on the cow and wolf tracks, reining only when necessary to stay on track. The stillness rose up around him, that stillness that comes when a man is totally alone in the wild, the stillness of ancient mountains and desolate regions where few men venture.

He rode onto a wide shelf of grassy land that was still moist from the runoff of a recent rain. The tracks were well-defined, and he read them as if they were headlines in a newspaper. The cow's hoofprints had drained of most of the moisture, while the wolf's were still wet, glistening in the light as if painted in quicksilver. The wolf had not started to run yet, and it was obvious that the cow had been snatching tufts of grass along the way, as if it had some predetermined destination in mind.

The shelf gradually sloped down to a swale thick with tall waving grasses and a tangle of berry bushes. He heard the cow before he saw her. She was bawling from somewhere down below, and he heard the snarl of the wolf, saw its movement through the high grass.

Brad yelled out and headed his horse toward the sound of the bawling cow. It was tough going, and the cow's cries grew louder. He rode up and felt his horse stumble. He heard the splash of water and the faint trickle of a stream. He saw the dam then, a beaver dam across a small stream. The cow was wallowing in deep water just below it, and the wolf was at her neck. Brad hauled in on the reins and dropped to the ground. He drew his pistol so fast, it was a dark blur. He took two steps and the wolf's head rose up for just a second. He saw the slavering jaws, the bloodlust in the wolf's feral eyes. He thumbed back the hammer on his single-action Colt .45 and the pistol roared, spitting sparks and flame. The wolf's head jerked with the impact of the lead ball, and the animal tumbled into the stream, turning the water crimson.

Brad slid the pistol back in its holster and took another step. The ground slid out from beneath him, and he heard the ominous sound of a rattlesnake, so loud he thought the sound was coming from inside his own head.

He slid into a deep hidden hole five yards from where the brindle cow was floundering to get out, and that's when he saw the coiled rattler atop a flat rock right next to the sinkhole. As he kept sliding toward the cow, the rattler struck, a scaled lightning bolt with its jaws open, fangs catching the sunlight, gleaming like surgical needles.

Brad lashed out a hand at the snake as it struck for his throat. The snake's mouth closed on his hand, burying its fangs in the soft flesh of the heel. Brad rolled over, grasping at the snake's head with his left hand, pinning its body beneath his leg. He pulled the head and fangs away from his hand, dug a thumb into its neck, a spot just behind its head, dug his fingernail into the scaly flesh, pushing, pushing inward with all of his strength, severing the hard crust of its skin until he dug into its flesh. He sawed back and forth with his thumbnail as the snake writhed beneath him, its tail, with its rattles, banging against his boot.

The brindle cow lurched from its wet sinkhole and lumbered off, with mud up over its hocks, bawling in terror as the sound of the snake's clattering rattles shattered the silence of the afternoon. Sunlight played in the tops of the trees, the pines dancing with hand shadows as Brad bore down with his thumb, burrowing deep into the snake's gullet, severing veins and gristle, choking off the serpent's airway, his hand soaked with fluid. He felt no pain from the bite. The snake struggled to break Brad's grip, turning its head so that Brad could see into its slitted yellow eyes, feel the forked tongue flicking against his fingers like something that crawled out of the night into a man's dreams, causing him to shiver with its malevolent electricity.

Brad slid his index finger from his left hand into the snake's mouth, pried its head back as he continued to crush its neck and drive his fingernail deeper into its rippling flesh. The snake thrashed and struggled, but the fangs lifted from the twin holes in the back of Brad's hand. The puslike venom continued to shoot out from its hollow fangs, a milky flow with a yellowish cast.

He pinched the snake's jaws together, held the head clamped between thumb and forefinger, then drew his knife from its scabbard. He severed the head from the body with one swipe, let the head fall to the ground between his legs. He took the knife and sliced a furrow between the two holes left by the snake's fangs, sheathed his knife and began to bunch up the skin around the new wound. Venom oozed from his hand. He shook it, squeezed it, then sucked out the small gouts he could still see around the twin holes.

He felt movement beneath him. The snake's body was still whipping and writhing, but the ground was also slipping down in a slow slide. He looked up behind him and saw the boulders beginning to move as well. One was teetering on a precarious perch. The ground was eroded, and there were rivulets of earth where once water had coursed. He slid even farther, and dropped the still wriggling snake and tried to turn over, claw his way out of the brush and loose shale.

His hand stung now, and he felt a numbness in his fingers. The sun was dipping ever lower behind the distant mountain peaks, the sky a pagan blaze of bronze and steel, flaring rays that torched the clouds as others turned to ocher dust and mourning ashes.

The boulders shifted and jostled against one another. The pebbles beneath him, caught by falling dirt and sand, slid down toward the depression in the earth. The first trickle became a torrent, and the boulders lost their footing and toppled. Gravity pulled at them, and they rumbled down, rolled and jumped like objects suddenly freed. The rocks crackled and boomed. A medium-sized boulder leaped into the air and came crashing down on Brad's head.

He felt the blow, the sharp sting as his scalp opened up, and then he saw an explosion of bright stars and the sunset smearing into a gaudy blur. He sank from consciousness like the very stone that struck him and descended into an obsidian abyss, a darkness so black it wrenched the stars from the sky and oblitered all light and color.

Brad floated in that fathomless deep of sleep, sinking ever downward into a peaceful sea of oblivion while the boulders rumbled into the small gully and came to rest under mangled branches, releasing the fragrance of crushed leaves and dank soil as the sun slid behind a distant snow-capped peak and the shadow of dusk spread across the land.

The brindle cow broke into a trot at the noise and stopped when it was over, panting, sides heaving, rubbery nose twitching. Alone in the spreading darkness, it lifted its head and bawled at the sky until nothing was left of its bellow but a low grunt of despair.

The cow was alone, and its taste for grass left somewhere on the hillside, far from its home.

THREE

❧

Felicity Storm stood on the front porch of the log house, staring up at the hills, the lowering sun. She was a firm, wiry woman with raven hair and hazel eyes, a patrician nose, the sculpted features of a Grecian goddess. But, there was a worried shadow flickering in her eyes as she spotted Julio driving cattle down to the pasture already filled with the grazing herd standing like statues in an ocean of grama grass. She wondered why Brad wasn't with Julio, and the worry lines around her eyes deepened as she squinted into the falling sun.

She stooped over, her simple cotton dress flowing with the bending of her knees, clinging to her girlish form like running water. She picked up the wicker basket and tucked it under one arm, glided down the steps until her sandals touched ground. She walked to the side of the house where the clothesline danced with the dried parchments of her washing: sheets, underclothes, shirts and blouses, linens, all white, like unmarred documents. She kept her eyes on the hillside beyond the driven cattle, searching for Brad. She thought he might be chasing in a stray and would appear at any moment, framed against the pines and spruce like a conquering warrior returning from a long journey.

Carlos Renaldo came around the side of the house lugging a burlap bag over one shoulder. He, too, was looking in Julio's direction, a worried frown on his face. He passed close to Felicity and stopped.

"I dug some potatoes for you," he said. "I will put them in the house."

"Just set them on the porch, Carlos. Did you get some for yourself?"

"Yes," he said. "Where is Brad? He is not with Julio, and Julio has the cows that ran away."

"I don't know," she said, lifting a pair of long johns from the line, folding them before putting them in the basket. "Maybe . . ."

She did not finish her thought because she saw the worry in Carlos's face. He worshipped her husband, she knew, and his concern was genuine. She bit her lip and scrunched up her face, wondering if she even had an idea of where Brad could be. If one of the cows strayed, she thought that he would surely send Julio to chase it down. That should be Brad driving the cows back to pasture, not Julio.

"I will take the potatoes," Carlos said, and went on his way toward the front porch.

Julio took off his hat and waved the cattle down into the pasture. The cows took off at a run and joined the grazing herd as if they were long-lost relatives returning to home and family.

The breeze stiffened, and Felicity saw the leaves on the birch trees jiggle and flash various shades of green down by the creek. The clothes flapped mindlessly on the line, sounding like a chorus of whips, and she grabbed a sheet that was beginning to slide off, rolled it into a ball, and dropped it into the basket. The breeze was warm at first, then began to cool as the sun's rim glowed fiery orange just above the mountain skyline to the west, painting the long stretch of clouds a pastel pink on their underbellies while their tops faded to an ashen gray. Shadows crawled along the valley, and the canyons blackened into deep repositories of soft coal.

Felicity quickly pulled all the dry clothes from the line and stuffed them in her basket as Julio rode up to her, his face gray with shadow, the blazing sunset at his back.

"Where's Brad?" she asked, a chunk of her heart caught in her throat, the remains pumping like a trip-hammer in her chest.

"He was following the track of the brindle cow. The cow, she strayed, and he went to get her." He looked back over his shoulder at the dark pines on the hilltop and beyond, into the unknown. "I think he will come back soon."

"How soon, Julio?"

"Very soon, I think. The cow could not have gone far."

"Why didn't you stay with him?"

"He told me to come on back."

He slid from the saddle and looked longingly toward the barn and the horse stalls.

"It's getting dark up there," she said.

"Brad can find his way."

"I know he can, and he always said the cows could find their way back home, too."

"Do not worry, Felicitas. Brad will be home soon. I will put the horse up, give him some water and grain."

"You don't think Brad ran into trouble up there?"

"There was nobody there but us. Why do you worry?"

"I worry because when Pilar went to fetch water from the creek this morning, she saw fresh horse tracks."

Pilar was Julio's wife. A look of startled surprise spread across his face as if he had been slapped with wet rawhide.

"Somebody was watching the house last night. Curly barked, but we didn't let him out."

Curly was the Storms' dog, part Irish setter, part mongrel of some unknown breed.

"That dog barks at everything."

"Brad went to the front window and looked outside for a long time. He didn't see or hear anything."

"He did not say nothing to me," Julio said.

"He wouldn't. When I asked him what Curly was barking at, he just said 'the moon.' But he got Curly to shut up."

"Did Brad see the horse tracks?"

"No."

"Did he go down to the creek?"

"As soon as he got up."

"And, he did not see them?"

"No, because the tracks were not there. I said they were fresh. Someone was watching the house after you and Brad went to find those strays."

"Maybe Indians giving their horses water to drink."

"These horses were shod, Julio."

"How many horses?"

"Only two that I could see."

She picked up the basket and started walking toward the front porch. Julio tied his reins to one of the clothesline poles and walked with her.

"Julio, I want you and Carlos to pack iron from now on."

"What do you say, Felicity?"

"Carry your pistol and a rifle. Both of you ride the tree line above and to the side of the house before dark. If you find any horse tracks, you come back and tell me."

"You think there will be trouble?"

"Friendly folk riding up here would have stopped to say howdy. Those tracks mean something. Something I don't like."

As she neared the porch, Curly began barking inside the house.

"People pass by," Julio said. Lamely.

"Not up here, they don't. Do what I say. I'm going to sit outside until it's dark and wait for Brad. If he doesn't come back tonight, we'll ride out in the morning and look for him."

"He will be here soon, I think."

When Felicity reached the porch, she stopped and turned around. Julio was still standing there.

"There's not much daylight left, Julio. I want to know what I'm facing here with Brad gone."

"Yes," Julio said, and turned to leave. "Do not worry, eh?"

"I won't worry. But I sure as shootin' want to be ready for anybody up to no good."

Julio left and Felicity went inside the house. Curly jumped up to greet her, and she motioned for him to sit. The dog sat, wagging its tail.

"You're not going to go out right now, Curly," she said, and walked past him into the bedroom. She set the basket of clothes on the floor, drew in a deep breath, and walked to the wardrobe. She opened the doors, reached up to the top shelf, and pulled down her pistol and holster. The belt, glistening with cartridges, was wrapped around the holster. She strapped on the pistol, drew it, and cocked it. She held her thumb on the hammer and spun the cylinder. It was full of unfired rounds. She squeezed the trigger and eased the hammer back down, seating it at half cock. Then she reached into the corner of the wardrobe and pulled out a Henry repeating rifle. She levered a shell into the chamber, hefted it. The magazine was full. She had thirteen cartridges ready to fire.

Brad had taught her to shoot, but she had never shot at a man. She had shot down elk and deer, antelope on the plains, and rabbits. She was pretty good with the scattergun, too, and had brought down quail and partridges on the wing.

Pilar let Curly out when she went outside. She sat in one of the chairs on the porch and watched the blazing sky in the west turn to ashes, the clouds like dusty smoke signals fading against the remnants of a glowing blue tapestry. She saw the first star wink on, Venus, just above the horizon, and the blackness of night came on. She listened, heard the chink of iron hooves on rocks as Carlos and Julio followed the tree line that encircled the ranch. She waited, knowing they would ride back soon, now that it was full dark.

Julio rode up to the porch, and she heard the muffled sounds of Carlos's horse as he made his way to the barn and stables.

His horse snorted as Julio reined up.

"Well?" she said.

"Yes, we saw horse tracks up where the trees are thick. Two horses. We saw where they stopped and smoked the cigarettes. Maybe they were looking at the house."

"Or counting cattle," she said.

"Maybe. Yes."

"You and Carlos will have to take turns," she said.

"Take turns?"

"As nighthawks. They might come back and steal some of our cows."

"Where? This is a long valley. The cows are many."

"I should have both of you out there, but if you see or hear anything, you shoot your rifle, Julio, and we'll come running. Saddle my horse and leave yours and Carlos's saddled."

"You think the riders are rustlers? We saw only two sets of horse tracks."

"Maybe they won't come tonight, but we can't take a chance. Brad would have a fit if anyone rustled our cattle."

"Perhaps he will ride in soon."

"I will wait for him until I get sleepy, Julio. Go and talk to Carlos. Do you want Curly to go with you?"

"Yes. He has a good nose and good ears. He would bark, I think."

"Call him. He's down in the pasture somewhere, picking up burrs and looking for rabbits."

"I will call him after I talk to Carlos and ride out to watch the herd. *Ten cuidado,* Felicity."

"I'll be careful," she said.

And then Julio was gone around the side of the house, heading toward the barn.

She sat and listened, wondering where Curly was, and then she looked up at the dark hills and her eyes misted.

Brad was out there somewhere, all alone, or hurt, perhaps, and . . .

She didn't want to think of anything else that might have happened to her husband. He was a careful man, but . . .

She listened to the silence, and it was a deep silence.

It was a lonesome silence that she had not felt in a long, long time.

FOUR

෪

The wiry Arapaho reached down and picked up the head-
less snake. He shook the tail, heard the rattles clack together. He slid the snake through his belt and let it dangle
against the left leg of his trousers. Then he rolled the
boulder off the white man's head and leaned down, putting his ear to the unconscious man's mouth. He felt the
faint puffs of air against his ear and grunted. He grabbed
the man's shoulders and pulled him away from the rock
slide, laid him flat on stationary ground.

The sky was turning to dust over the western snowcaps,
but there was a glimmer of salmon light still clinging to
the horizon. He lifted the limp man by the shoulders and
slung him over his back and walked up the slope to the
fringe of pine trees. He entered the woods on silent moccasins, carrying the white man with ease. His legs were
strong and his shoulders broad. His black hair hung in a
pigtail down his shirted back. He followed a game trail to
a hut where another man, a Hopi with graying black hair,
stood like a sentinel outside the shelter, his dark eyes
shimmering with the last of the day's light.

"Did you catch the snake?" the Hopi asked.

The Arapaho reached down and jiggled the dead rattler. It made a *brrr* sound like tiny bones shaking in an iron kettle.

"That is the one?"

"That is the one that ran away when I opened the basket."

"Too bad. It was the sidewinder I brought to you."

"I know. It was good medicine."

"It is still good medicine," the Hopi said.

The Arapaho walked past the Hopi and laid the white man on a buffalo robe, then stepped back outside into the twilight. He pulled the dead snake from his belt and held it up for the Hopi to see.

"Why did you kill the snake?"

"I did not kill the snake. The white man bit its head off."

"You saw him do this?"

"No. But, the head is gone. Maybe the white eyes swallowed it."

"Let us see," the Hopi said.

The two entered the shelter. They had woven stripped saplings together and used spruce bows to shed the rain. There was a smoke hole in the top of the dome, and a ring of stones in the center, with hot coals and kindling stacked nearby. The shelter was full of woven baskets, and from some of them, sounds of slithering seeped out, the rustle of scales and soft hisses. The Hopi squatted down and lifted the white man's hands. He rubbed his hand over the backs of them and then turned them over, touching the palms with his fingertips.

"He has been bitten by the snake," the Hopi said. He drew his knife from its antelope skin sheath and began to slice across the holes made by the snake's fangs. Blood and creamy venom oozed from the fresh wounds.

The Hopi lifted the wounded man's hand to his face and opened his mouth. He put his lips over the two holes and the cuts he had made in the flesh and sucked hard, his ruddy cheeks collapsing as he drew out the poison. He spat to the side and sucked the wounds again. He spit out the venom and blood.

"Make fire," the Hopi said to the Arapaho.

The Arapaho grunted in assent. He pulled a box of lucifers from his leather pouch, struck one of the matches on a stone. He held the lighted match to the shavings beneath a small pyramid of shaved sticks and the shavings began to smoke. A tiny flame appeared and the Arapaho fanned it gently with one hand. The fire erupted from the kindling and the blaze spread. He put sticks on the fire and the shelter glowed a soft orange as the fresh wood caught fire.

"Now we can see," the Hopi said, "and we will be warm in the night."

"Yes," the Arapaho said, and sat next to the white man, studying his face. He passed a hand over Brad's closed eyelids, and they seemed to flutter in the firelight.

He touched the top of Brad's head where the falling rock had struck him. He felt the wetness and the stickiness of blood. He put the finger to his lips and tasted the blood. There was a lump on the white man's head, and it was soft and sticky with oozing blood.

He pulled Brad's pistol from his holster, felt its heft. He lifted it up so that the blued barrel gleamed in the firelight. He turned it around in his hand.

"Do you take his little firestick?" the Hopi asked.

"No. I just like to see it and feel it in my hand. It is a very fine little firestick."

"It has six killer bees in it," the Hopi said.

"Yes. I know. I have seen many in the hands of white men."

He slid the pistol back in its holster and picked up a wooden canteen. He poured water over the lump on Brad's head and rubbed the blood away and into his scalp. Then he poked Brad in the side to see if he could rouse him from his sleep.

Brad did not stir, but a small moan escaped from his lips.

"He sleeps much," the Arapaho said. "Maybe he will die from the snake's spit."

"No, he will not die," the Hopi said. "The poison will make him strong. He will be like the snake."

The Hopi cut the rattles from the snake's tail. He shook them and smiled into the firelight.

"Strong medicine," he said.

The Arapaho grunted. "What do you do?" he asked the Hopi.

"I will make a little hole in the rattle and put a leather string through it so the white man can wear it around his neck."

"He will not like it."

"It will make him strong," the Hopi said.

"My heart is bad because I let the snake get away. It just crawled from the basket and did not rattle. By the time I looked inside, he was gone from the hut. I hunted him, but he found the white man before I could catch him."

"We can still take the other snakes back to your village and make the ground shake with our feet."

"You carried the snake that crawls sideways, the one the white man calls the sidewinder, from far away. My heart is on the ground because he got away." The Arapaho's forehead wrinkled, and he squinted through a taciturn scowl.

The Hopi began to work on the set of rattles. The Arapaho scooted over to the dead snake, laid it on a flat rock, took his knife out, and began to skin it. He put the meat into a clay bowl as he scraped it away from the inner side of the skin. The two worked in silence as the fire began to glow with just enough light to see. Stars appeared over the smoke hole, winking through the gauze of smoke like diamonds in a murky stream.

The two men cooked the snake meat and ate it slowly,

chewing on each roasted piece and rubbing their bellies when they were through.

"The white man awakens," the Hopi said when he got up to go outside and relieve himself.

The Arapaho looked at Brad and saw his eyelids quiver.

"He still sleeps," he said.

But by the time the Hopi came back inside, Brad's eyes were blinking and he had raised one hand over his face.

"He sleeps with his eyes open," the Hopi said.

The Arapaho laughed. "Huh," he grunted. "Most white men sleep with their eyes open. They have much fear of the red man."

The Hopi laughed at that and sat down next to Brad, looking at him with interest.

The Arapaho moved over on the other side of the white man and watched him awaken.

"He looks at his hand," the Hopi said. "He wonders if the biting snake was a dream."

"Let us speak in his tongue, Gray Owl," the Arapaho said in English. "Maybe he will make talk with us."

"You are very wise, Wading Crow. But what if he is French? Do you speak that tongue?"

"I speak the bad words in that tongue, Gray Owl."

"I speak some of the good words of the French."

"Ho, you brag, Gray Owl. You thump your chest but I hear only the English."

"Where am I?" Brad asked, sitting up. He touched his head gingerly, winced at the sudden sharp pain. He seemed to have difficulty focusing on the two men on either side of him, and the fire had burned down so much he could not see their faces clearly.

"You are here, white man," Wading Crow said. "What are you called?"

"Oh, my name. I am called Brad Storm. Last thing I remember was getting bit by a rattlesnake."

"You do not know the mountain fell on you?" Wading Crow smiled at Gray Owl.

"My head hurts like hell," Brad said. Then he held up his hand and looked at it, saw the cuts and the two holes.

"Let us name him Sidewinder," Gray Owl said. "The white man's name is like dry corn in my mouth."

Wading Crow pointed a finger at Brad.

"We call you Sidewinder," he said in his guttural English.

Brad pointed to the Arapaho.

"You Wading Crow," he said. "Me Sidewinder. Good enough?"

"And I am called Gray Owl," the Hopi said. "You Sidewinder."

Brad felt dizzy, but he also felt as if he had made two friends. He did not ask about the snakes he heard buzzing in their baskets, and he did not ask about his horse. He thought of Felicity just before he fell asleep. The night was so dark he knew he could not find his way home.

He dreamed of tracking a large white cow that walked through a field of snakes, and his head throbbed like a drummer's tambour as he sank deeper into slumber.

One of the Indians snored, but Brad didn't know which one.

FIVE

❦

Felicity felt as if she had slept on a pile of boards during the night. She awoke with stiffness in her joints, small stabbing pains in her back and neck, and a slight headache. She hadn't had much sleep, and the little she got was shallow and disturbed by wild dreams about looking for Brad in endless canyons that were like a maze.

Neither of their hands had seen anything the night before, nor had she. Perhaps she was making a mountain out of a molehill, she thought, as she boiled a pot of Arbuckles coffee and water. She looked out the kitchen window to see the light of dawn crack the eastern horizon, and later, when she sat on the back porch sipping the coffee, the sky was scarlet, a raging portent of bad weather to come.

The morning air was sweet and clean. The few head of cattle around the house were just rising from their beds, and Felicity could smell their scent wafting her way on the morning breeze, a pungent aroma of hide and cow pies, earth and crushed vegetation. She wished Brad were sitting beside her, sipping coffee, describing what he saw with those piercing eyes of his. She missed him terribly and was worried that he might be injured. Or dead.

The thought froze her face and hollowed out her insides. She suddenly felt queasy and fought to keep the tears from welling up in her eyes. It was early, but in that moment she knew what she must do and she made her decision. Soon, she knew, Julio would walk down to the back porch and ask her what she wanted him to do that day. Nothing was as urgent, in her mind, as the task of finding Brad and bringing him back home.

The eastern sky blazed in the morning stillness, and her coffee was cooling. She drank the last in her cup and stood up, stretched. She was dressed for the day and wore her pistol in its leather holster. Her rifle was just inside the back door, but as she looked across the field to the timber, she saw nothing out of the ordinary. A few minutes later, she heard the crunch of Julio's boots as he walked down from the bunkhouse along a narrow path filled with loose pebbles. It was a comforting sound, and she set her empty cup on the railing and waited for him to turn the corner and come into view.

"*Buenos días,* Felicity," Julio said, as he walked around the corner of the house.

"Had breakfast, Julio?"

"Yes. I have already saddled the horses."

"Mine, too?"

"Yes. I think you will want to come with me to find Brad."

"You read my mind, Julio."

He laughed and put a booted foot on the bottom step of the porch stairs.

"I'll put my cup away, and we'll go look for Brad."

"I will wait," he said.

She returned in a few moments, carrying her rifle and a box of .44 cartridges. She also carried a wrapped bundle under her arm. She handed this to Julio.

"Sandwiches," she said.

"You come prepared," Julio said.

"We might get hungry," she said.

"I mean the *cartuchos*," he said, pointing to the cartridges in her hand.

"There are cougars up there, and bears."

"The wolves, too."

"I doubt if we'll see any wolves this morning."

They walked to the barn. Carlos came out to meet them, leading their horses.

"Did you see or hear anything last night, Carlos?" Felicity asked.

"No, I hear nothing," he said in his thick Mexican accent. "The cows, they sleep good, I think. It was very quiet. I sleep with one ear open."

He grinned and Felicity grinned back at him. She took the reins and mounted her horse, a bay mare she called Rose. Julio climbed aboard his horse, Chato. She noticed that Julio's rifle was in its saddle scabbard.

"Canteens full, Julio?" she asked.

"Yes. From the spring."

"Let's go," she said. "Carlos, keep on eye on the cattle."

"*Seguro,*" Carlos said.

Julio and Felicity rode toward the hills bordering the valley. He was looking to his left at the clumps of cattle heading toward the grasses in the sunlight, those with the dew burned off by the morning sun. He stopped and pointed to a lone cow walking briskly toward some others.

"What is it?" she said, pulling up alongside him.

"There is the brindle cow," he said.

"The brindle cow?"

"That is the one Brad was finding."

"Are you sure?" She shaded her eyes so that she could see the cow more clearly.

"Yes. I am sure."

"Then, maybe Brad is right behind her. It looks as if she is just now getting back from wherever she's been."

Julio looked up toward the trees, the top of the hill they

had to climb. Felicity looked up there, too. They were silent for several moments.

"I do not see him," he said.

"Well, maybe we'll see him when we get up there."

"Maybe," he said, but his voice held no conviction.

They rode into the timber, following the path Julio and Brad had ridden the day before, a path still littered with cow tracks, a maze of cuneiform wedges in the soft spring earth. Felicity could see that the tracks went both ways.

Brad had taught her to track, and she studied the hoof marks as they rode through thin timber, climbing ever so slowly. She saw two sets of horseshoe tracks heading up and one set heading back down toward the ranch. Julio, she knew, had made those when he drove the strays back onto the ranch pasture. Her heart felt squeezed when she saw them, deciphered their meaning.

They reached the small mesa where the cows had first strayed. Julio pointed out where the cattle had been, and the direction in which the brindle cow had gone when Brad began tracking it. She also noticed the burned ruins of the house that had once stood there. Julio told her the same story he had related to Brad and she sighed at the images she saw in her mind. The ruins looked so forlorn, and she found it hard to imagine how anyone could be so cruel as to kill an entire family over a few head of cattle.

Julio rode off as she sat there on her horse, lost in thought.

"The tracks are still here," he said, and Felicity turned to look at him, jarred out of her solemn reverie.

"Wait," she called. "I'm coming."

Julio pointed to the tracks of the brindle cow and the hoof marks of Brad's horse. He pointed in the direction where the cow had gone.

A few minutes later, she saw the wolf tracks and halted Julio.

"Were those made yesterday?" she said, pointing to the wolf tracks.

"I think so. Brad he no say anything."

"Well, if the wolf was following that cow, Brad must have seen it."

"Maybe," he said, and she felt like slapping Julio.

"He didn't say anything to you about the wolf?"

"No, he don't say nothing," Julio said, in his broken English.

"Brad could be hurt," she said, an urgency in her voice.

The two followed the tracks off the shelf and along the path the cow had taken. The horses had trouble following the sidehill. The trail had dried since the day before, but there were places where the trail was slippery. Felicity silently cursed the slowness of the horses, but thought about Brad and wondered if his horse might have fallen. She scanned the slope ahead and down into the steep canyon, looking for any sign of her husband.

The sun was well up when they came to the thicket where the brindle had gone. Both of them saw the jumble of rocks, the treacherous lay of the land in that spot.

"Maybe we should walk over there," Julio said. "Maybe we can read the tracks."

"Where is he?" Felicity cried out in frustration.

Julio did not answer.

They dismounted and ground-tied their horses to small bushes. They walked over to the thicket where the cow tracks disappeared. There was a maze of prints in the soft ground, including the wolf's, Brad's horse. As they walked around it, Felicity squatted down.

"Look here, Julio," she said. "What is this?" She pointed to a smeared track the size of a man's foot.

Julio squatted beside her and studied the track.

"*Indio*," he said.

"An Indian? What's an Indian doing up here?"

Julio said nothing. She could see that he was uncomfortable. He looked scared. And now that she thought about it, she felt scared, too.

"There is blood on the rocks," he said.

The two walked above the site, studying the ground.

Felicity was trying to form a picture in her mind. She saw drag marks that might have been made by Brad's body. It appeared the Indian had found him, pulled him out of the depression, and then lifted him onto his back. There were no drag marks above the small landslide and the moccasin tracks were deeper, more defined.

"That Indian carried him off, Julio," she said. "That's what I think."

"Maybe. I do not read the tracks so good."

"Yes, you do. I don't need to be mollycoddled. If Brad was hurt, maybe—"

Julio said something under his breath. Felicity was sure he said "*Indios*." She knew he had a fear of them. Past memories, she supposed.

"Let's get back on our horses and follow those tracks," she said. "They go right up into the timber."

Julio hesitated. She gave him a sharp look.

Felicity bristled at his apparent cowardice.

"*Tienes miedo?*" she said in Spanish. "Are you afraid?"

"Maybe we should get help."

"Where? There's no help anywhere near here. Brad may need us. If you're afraid, go on back to the ranch. I'll find him, wherever he is."

"I do not have fear," he said. "But it could be dangerous."

"Living is dangerous, Julio. I don't give a hoot. I'm going to find Brad if it takes me a week."

They got on their horses and were starting to ride up into the timber when they both saw movement off to their left. They both stopped and looked at the small shape coming from a long way off. As it drew nearer, they both could see that it was a horse and rider.

"Isn't that Brad's horse?" Felicity whispered, hardly daring to breathe.

"Yes, I think that is Brad's horse."

"Is that Brad?"

She stood up in the stirrups and waved her hand at the figure on the horse. On Brad's horse.

The man did not wave back. She settled back down in the saddle.

"Who is that?" she murmured, more to herself than to Julio.

"*Indio*," Julio said under his breath.

And Felicity felt her blood run cold as a hollow pit opened in her stomach and goose bumps rippled up her arms.

A cloud passed across the sun and she felt a sudden chill.

SIX

The squawk of a jay outside the wickiup roused Brad from his sleep. He opened his eyes to darkness and confusion. He heard the bird as it rustled leaves and pine needles, scratched the ground just outside the opening of the shelter. He felt a weight on his body, a blanket of some kind. He felt the covering with one hand, felt the fur, and wondered where he was for a long moment. His head ached and one of his hands felt as if it had been clawed by a wildcat. It stung, and when he touched it, he felt a sudden sharp pain. The pain made him suddenly sick to his stomach, and he fought to keep down the bile that rose in his throat.

He felt his now-swollen hand and shoots of pain coursed up his arm. He felt woozy and lay there for several moments until he saw a sliver of cream light break to the east, sending in shafts of shadows. Now he could hear the scurrying of chipmunks outside the lodge, and the sky began to take on a crimson hue. He looked around, hoping to discover where he was. His memory was locked somewhere in the dregs of dream and in the pain that gripped his hand and arm, in the boiling gases of his stomach.

Gradually, as the light crept into the shelter, he began to remember. He pulled himself up, pushing down the buffalo robe that covered him. As memory began to return, seeping into his consciousness, he expected to see the two forms of the Indians he had met the night before. He squinted and could make out only one sleeper, and the Indian was stirring, slipping off his buffalo robe, and stretching both arms to the smoke hole and the paling sky.

It was Gray Owl, the Hopi, and before Brad could say anything, the red man was on his feet and standing over Brad, his face in darkness.

"You wake," Gray Owl said.

"Just barely," Brad said.

"Huh?"

Brad didn't know whether the sound was a question or a grunt of assent.

"Bear?" Gray Owl said.

"*Un poco*," Brad said in Spanish.

"Ahhh," Gray Owl said. "Do you have hunger?"

Brad sat up, rubbed his stomach.

"Sick," he said. "*Enfermo. Mi estómago.*"

"Ah, it is the bite of the snake," Gray Owl said in Spanish.

Brad saw his pistol lying next to where he had slept. It was in its holster. He touched the top of his head, very gingerly, looked around again to see if he had missed anything that might be his.

"What you look for?" Gray Owl asked in English.

"My hat. I was wearing a hat."

"Ah, no hat. You no need hat. Let the sun cure your head, Sidewinder."

Sidewinder. That was the name the Indians had given him.

"Where is Wading Crow?" he asked.

Gray Owl walked outside, stared at the fiery sky of morning.

"Wading Crow get horse."

"My horse?"

"Yes. He track horse, bring horse back. Give you horse."

Brad jumped when he heard a rattle from one of the baskets. At that moment, Gray Owl turned and saw him.

The Hopi grinned.

"Rattlesnakes," Brad said, and it wasn't a question. There was no mistaking that sound. Other snakes began to rattle, and Brad scanned the floor to see if any had gotten loose.

"I have gift for Sidewinder," Gray Owl said as he walked back into the shelter.

"I hope it's not a rattler," he said.

Gray Owl walked to his robe and reached underneath it. He pulled out something, wadded it up in his hand, and walked back to Brad, who was still nervous over the snakes. Gray Owl opened his hand.

Brad stared down at a set of rattles. Attached to them was a thin strand of sinew.

"Take," Gray Owl said. "Wear here." He raised his hand and pointed to his neck.

"What for?" Brad asked, taking the rattle necklace.

"Bring good luck to Sidewinder. I cut from snake you killed. Snake that bite you."

"I killed the snake that had these rattles?"

Gray Owl nodded. He signed that Brad should wear the necklace.

Brad put it on.

"You get in trouble, you shake rattle. Good luck."

He felt funny wearing the rattles, but Gray Owl had saved his life, most probably. Brad would wear the necklace as long as he was there.

"Why do you have all these snakes in baskets, Gray Owl?"

"Sit," Gray Owl said. "I tell Sidewinder a story."

They sat opposite each other, the fire ring between them. Gray Owl put some kindling on the coals and stirred them with another stick. He blew into the coals. They flared and ignited the kindling. As he talked, he added more sticks to the fire.

"Snakes for Snake Dance," Gray Owl said. "Wading Crow good friend. I bring sidewinder from my hunting grounds. We catch snakes in mountains. Take to village, dance the Snake Dance of my people."

"Who are your people?"

"I am Hopi. My people the Summer People of the Hopi."

"You dance with live snakes?" Brad was dumbfounded. He had never heard of such a thing.

"Big medicine," Gray Owl said.

"Why?"

"Tell story. You listen."

"I'm listening," Brad said. His hand and his arm had stopped hurting, and his stomach was no longer roiling. He fingered the rattles around his neck. He liked the smooth bony feel of them. They seemed to have a calming effect on him.

Gray Owl's face danced with fire and shadow as he spoke, and his eyes looked like polished black agates.

"Many robe seasons ago, a father of the Summer People and his son had bad words about the offerings made for our gods. The son told his father that he did not believe there were any gods. He did not believe the gods took the offerings and ate them. He said the offerings just rotted away. The father said that there were gods and that they ate the offerings.

"The son said he would go to the Lower Place and find out for himself if there were any gods. The father and the Wise Ones told the boy that the gods did not actually eat the food offerings. They took from them the core, what is the heart-meaning of the offering."

"The essence," Brad murmured, caught up in the story.

Gray Owl nodded.

"The boy did not believe his father or the Wise Ones, and he left the village. As he was walking along, he met the Silent One, a Tewa rain god. The Silent One said to the boy: 'Where are you going?' The boy answered, 'I am going to the Lower Place to look for the gods.' The Silent

One told the boy, 'You cannot go there. Even if you walk until your hair is white as the snows and your teeth fall out, you will never get there. It is too far. Go back to your village. The gods are real. Do not have doubt that there are gods.'

"After telling the boy this, the Silent One changed himself into a god. He was like smoke and mist and cloud. The boy looked at the Silent One in his god form with wonder and fear. Then the Silent One made himself into a man once again, eh? And the boy was even more shaken. He was like a little tree in the wind. He shook and shook."

Gray Owl paused and stirred the fire. It was now warm inside the rustic hut, even as the cool breeze of morning breathed a chill into the air.

"Did the boy go back to his village?" Brad asked.

"No. He had a stiff backbone. He went on. He wanted to find out if there were truly gods. He did not believe there were any gods."

"Stubborn," Brad said.

Gray Owl made no comment. Instead, he continued with his story.

"So, the boy continued his journey to the Lower Place. He met Deer-Kachina-Cloud, another god who was in human form. Gods could do that. The god scolded the boy, and told him to turn around and go back home. The boy would not and Deer-Kachina-Cloud became angry. 'I have horns,' the god said. 'I am the gamekeeper for your people.' Then Deer-Kachina-Cloud changed into his god form and the boy saw the horns and the deer hooves and the face with much hair, and he had much fear from the snorting and the scraping of hooves on the ground. Then the god changed back into man form. The boy said he was going on to the Lower Place. Deer-Kachina-Cloud told him that he was near Snake Village. 'Go there,' Deer-Kachina-Cloud told the boy, 'after you go there, you go back home.'"

Gray Cloud stopped and took a deep breath. He looked up through the smoke hole and closed his eyes.

"Did the boy do what he promised?" Brad asked.

"Ah, do you think a boy like that would give up the hunt?"

"I don't reckon," Brad said. "But he did promise, didn't he?"

"Ah, yes, the boy did promise the god that he would visit Snake Village and then go back to his village."

"So, what did the boy do?"

"As he was walking toward Snake Village, another god in man form stopped him. This was Star-Flickering-Glossy Man. He was dressed in a coat made of many bird feathers. He warned the boy again and told him he could go only to Snake Village. 'Go no farther,' he said, and gave the boy a little twig with leaves. 'The snakes will try to bite you because you are a doubter. This herb will protect you. Shake it, show it to the snakes. In the center of the village there is the head man. Go to him. Go to him quick. The snakes are also spirits, and they can change into men. You will be in much danger.'"

Gray Owl stopped, and looked long and hard at Brad.

"This is a long story," Gray Owl said. "You may not be ready to hear the rest of it."

"I would like to hear it all, but I'm thinking I'd better get on home. My wife will be worried."

"Maybe she looks for you," Gray Owl said.

"Maybe."

"Wading Crow will return soon. I will tell you the rest of the story another time."

"How long will you be here? Have you got enough snakes?"

"We need thirty," Gray Owl said, and he made the sign, opening and closing his hands three times, extending his fingers when hands were open. "We only have twenty. No, one less, now that the sidewinder is in the spirit world."

"I'm sorry I killed your snake," Brad said.

"You killed so you would not be killed. That is all a man can do."

"I am not as sick as I should be. You got much of the poison out, I think."

"The poison was not much. Only a little got into your body."

"I am grateful. Thank you."

"That sidewinder was not meant for the dance. It made a journey to you, and you killed it. You took its medicine and now you have it in you. The rattles will help you overcome your enemies. They are good medicine."

"I believe they just might be," Brad said.

Gray Owl got to his feet.

"Believe," he said in a solemn tone. "Believe and the gods will watch over you."

Brad said nothing, but he felt the weight of the Hopi's words. A man could be what he wanted to be. Doubt was the enemy. He wondered if the Hopi boy, the doubter, would come to a bad end.

He could hardly wait to hear the rest of Gray Owl's story. He stood up and walked outside, breathing in the air, the scent of spruce and pine. Jays squabbled in the trees and chipmunks darted away from him, tails quivering, tiny squeakings issuing from their mouths. The snakes had stopped rattling, and the sun was rising still higher in the sky.

He flexed the snakebit hand. It worked just fine, he thought, and his head was returning to normal. He walked back inside and picked up his holstered pistol, strapped it on.

"I'm almost dressed," he told Gray Owl, who was cutting up meat for stew. "I might have to buy a new hat is all."

"Let your hair grow long, Sidewinder," Gray Owl said. "That is all the hat you need."

Gray Owl flicked his braids at Brad and grinned.

SEVEN

❧

Felicity's eyes narrowed to twin slits as she stared hard at the approaching rider.

"Are you sure that's not Brad?" she said to Julio. "That's Brad's roan, Ginger, sure as I'm looking at him. See that blaze on Ginger's forehead?"

"I see it," Julio said. "It looks like the roan gelding."

"And it looks like Brad's hat. He must be hurt. He looks so . . . so small."

"He is small," Julio said. "That is not Brad. That is an *indio*."

In the clear mountain air, Felicity could see a long way, but it was difficult to judge distances. The rider was still almost a mile away, maybe half a mile, and when he turned his head, she could plainly see Brad's grease- and sweat-mottled gray Stetson on the man's head. But, was it Brad? Her heart was starting to plummet in her chest as the rider slowly came closer.

She stood up in her stirrups and waved again.

"Brad, Brad," she shouted at the top of her voice. "Over here. Over here."

She waved and the rider raised an arm. Just raised it. The rider did not wave. Brad would have waved. He would have called to her. Her heart finished its plunge, and she could hear its rapid beating in her eardrum.

"That is not Brad," Julio said, and gripped the stock of his rifle as if to pull it from its boot.

"No, Julio," Felicity said, "don't you dare shoot that man."

"I will not shoot," he said, letting the rifle slide back a few inches. "I will be ready to shoot."

"Did you see him wave back at me?" she asked.

"He raised his arm."

"Maybe he's hurt."

Julio said nothing. He continued to stare at the rider, and he kept his hand on the stock of his rifle.

Brad's horse was picking its way along an ill-defined game trail that was rocky and treacherous. The gelding tossed its head every few steps, flaring its mane, its tail switching at deer flies, its steps careful and, to Felicity, painfully slow.

"Brad," she called again.

The rider did not answer, and with her heart sinking even more into that netherworld of fear and anxiety, she knew the rider was not her husband.

As Ginger came closer, Felicity saw the rider's face. It was a dark face, and the sun glinted off polished leather the color of burgundy. High cheekbones, straight black hair, a deerskin tunic, elk-hide trousers. Moccasins in the stirrups. Beaded moccasins. A knife at his belt. There was also something tucked into his belt about belly button high, some kind of leather pouch, she thought. It had loops in it and a leather drawstring. She supposed it was a kind of possibles pouch carried inside his trousers. She had never seen a full-blood Indian this close before. He looked fearsome, and she was still not sure if he could be trusted.

"His face is not painted," Julio breathed in what sounded to Felicity like a sigh of relief.

"No," she said tightly.

The Arapaho reined Ginger in some ten yards from where Felicity and Julio sat their horses.

"Where is my husband?" Felicity asked.

"You are the woman of Brad Storm?" Wading Crow asked.

"I am his wife, yes."

"I catch his horse."

"I can see that. What have you done with my husband? With Brad?"

"You come. You follow."

Wading Crow turned Ginger off the trail and headed for higher ground.

"Where are you taking us?" Felicity demanded, spurring her horse to catch up with the Arapaho.

"Take to Brad," Wading Crow answered.

Felicity looked over at Julio, who was trying to flank Wading Crow. He shrugged.

"Is it far?" Felicity asked, an anxiousness in her voice that betrayed her doubts.

"No far," Wading Crow answered.

She looked at Brad's hat on Wading Crow's head. It was battered and scuffed, and she thought she saw red stains on the underside of the brim. Blood, she thought. Brad's blood.

"Is . . . is my husband hurt?" she asked. She could see the Arapaho up close now. His expression was taciturn. Like the iron in the mountains, it was reddish and brown at the same time, an ancient mask that brought up stories she had heard as a girl about the savage behavior of the Indian. An involuntary shudder coursed through her, and she fought to keep her emotions from showing.

Wading Crow did not answer right away, and Felicity resisted the urge to pound on her saddle horn with a balled-up fist.

"Husband good," he said. "Rattlesnake bite him. Gray Owl suck out poison."

"Are you Gray Owl?" she said.

"Me Wading Crow."

She had the feeling that Wading Crow was deliberately talking to her as if he knew only a few words of English. She suspected he could talk better than he did.

"Is that blood on Brad's hat?" she asked, pointing to her own brim.

"Blood yes. Rock fall on Brad. Break head."

"His head is broken?"

"Little broke," Wading Crow said in that same, exasperating laconic tone of voice. She wanted to shake him, make him open up and tell her everything that had happened to Brad.

Wading Crow rode Brad's horse zigzag up the steep slope, avoiding the rocky, unstable area where the landslide had occurred. There were deep fissures all along the slope, gouged out by the melting snows, the spring runoff, and recent rains. Wisely, he let Ginger pick his way, find his footing, only using the reins to turn him back away from the more treacherous footing.

Clouds billowed out from behind the range to the north and west, great white thunderheads that blew slowly in their direction. Julio caught Felicity's attention and pointed to them.

"*Va a llover*," he said. "Much rain soon."

"Oh, I do hope we get back home with Brad before that storm catches us up here. Do you know where he's taking us?"

Julio shook his head. His forehead wrinkled with worry as he kept glancing up at the clouds.

They neared the top of the ridge, when Wading Crow held up his hand. He reined up and turned the horse to face Julio and Felicity.

"Why are we stopping?" she asked. "Are we close to where Brad is?"

Wading Crow touched a finger to his lips. He dismounted and handed the reins to Julio.

"*Espérate aquí*," he said to Julio in a low voice.

Felicity understood him.

"Why does he want us to wait here?" she asked Julio. "What's he going to do?"

Again, Julio shrugged, his face a blank.

Wading Crow reached into one of Brad's saddlebags and pulled out a forked stick, less than a foot long. The stick, cut from a juniper limb, was thick, the two ends sharpened to a point. He crouched low and began to stalk something neither Julio or Felicity could see. They both looked at each other in puzzlement.

Then they both heard the rattle a few yards ahead of Wading Crow. Both stiffened in their saddles. Felicity brought up her hand to her mouth as if to stifle a scream.

Julio's eyes widened. Felicity felt a shiver ripple up her spine. She had heard such rattles before, and she had a terrible fear of snakes. Brad had taught her to freeze and make no sudden movements.

"If you don't threaten a rattler, he'll run off eventually. If you get too close, the snake will strike. If you do get bit, just walk away and be calm. Otherwise, you'll speed up the poison."

She had never been bitten, but every time she heard a rattlesnake, she followed Brad's advice and just froze stock-still. As he had said, the snake would stop rattling, and she would see it slither away. But the fear was there, deep inside her, and she wondered why the Indian was going after one with that forked stick.

Wading Crow crouched even lower and moved so slowly it seemed to take him hours to make a single step. He paused after each step but moved ever closer. The rattling got louder the closer he got to the snake.

Finally, he stopped and very slowly straightened up. He raised the forked stick even more slowly and just stood there, staring at the ground. Neither Julio or Felicity could see the snake. But they could hear it.

Wading Crow inched closer to the spot where he focused his attention. One inch. Two. Then another. Then he drew in a breath and held it. His arm came down so fast that it was a blur, and he drove the stick into the ground. Then he pounced and the rattling became more frantic. He drove a hand straight down into the grass, his left hand, and knelt down. When his hand reappeared, he was holding a timber rattler, less than a foot long. It was fat and squirmed in Wading Crow's grip, lashing one way then another. He pulled the forked stick from the ground and began walking back to where Julio and Felicity were waiting, their hearts pounding like trip-hammers.

Felicity recoiled when Wading Crow got close. She closed her eyes and swallowed a scream. The horses grew nervous and tried to bolt or skitter away from the sound of danger. Julio and Felicity both pulled hard on the reins, the bits cutting into the horses' mouths and tongues, forcing their heads downward.

Wading Crow put the stick back in the saddlebag, then pulled the leather pouch out of his belt and worked the opening larger. He held the sack beneath the snake and watched it. He was holding the rattler just behind its head. Its mouth was open, and the fangs dripped venom as it struggled to free itself.

At the right moment, Wading Crow plunged the snake down into the bag and let the bag droop as he held onto the drawstring. The opening closed, and Wading Crow squeezed the top and pulled the drawstring tight.

Felicity felt faint. Her heart pounded, and her temples throbbed with rushing blood.

Julio's hand shook as he handed the reins to Wading Crow.

The bag shook with the snake's thrashings. Wading Crow tied the drawstring into a tight knot, then put it in the saddlebag next to the forked stick.

He mounted Brad's horse as if he had just stopped at a spring for a drink of water.

"We go," he said, and headed up toward the timber.

"What does he want with a snake?" Felicity asked Julio. "My god, what if it had gotten loose?"

Julio shrugged.

"Maybe he is going to eat it," he said.

Felicity shuddered again, then drew in a long breath.

In the distance, she could hear a faint rumble of thunder.

And the white clouds moved closer like a fleet of sailing ships. Behind them, more clouds, and their undersides were dark as if they had been dusted with charcoal.

High above them, a hawk sailed down into the valley, its head moving from side to side as it hunted below a blue sky, its wings burnished golden by the sun.

EIGHT

∾

Gray Owl filled a small clay bowl with warm roots, dried venison, and a thick broth. He handed the bowl to Brad.

"You eat," he said, signing with fingers to his own mouth.

"My belly feels pretty rocky."

"Eat. Good. Keep bad hand down. Hand get small again."

Brad took the bowl with his right hand, letting his left arm dangle. It made sense, he thought. The snake venom would stay close to his hand until it disappeared. The main thing, he thought, was to keep his hand below his heart. He knew that much from talking to men who had been snakebit. He gathered that Wading Crow had carried him here with his hand hanging low since the poison hadn't gone up his arm. What venom had been in his hand had been mostly sucked out by Gray Owl. He felt he was a very lucky man.

He put the bowl between his legs and dipped his right hand into the food, drew it to his mouth. It tasted odd.

"Chew slow," Gray Owl said.

Brad chewed slowly and swallowed the food. It seemed that he could feel its energy once it hit his stomach.

"Are you going to tell me the rest of that story, Gray Owl?"

"Good story. Heap more story."

Brad continued eating, a bite at a time, as Gray Owl ate and talked at the same time.

"The boy go to the Snake Village. Many snakes attack the boy. He chew the herb and spit at the snakes. They run away. Boy goes to Snake Chief. Snake Chief good to the boy, but say he go home. Walk no more to the Lower Place.

"Snake Chief have two daughters. The boy sleeps with one that night. Next day, he say he go back home. Snake Chief offer one of two daughters to boy. He take girl he sleep with. He . . . ah . . ."

"Choose?" Brad said.

"Yes. He choose girl he have under the blanket. Snake Chief, he marry girl and boy. Chief tell boy to make piki bread. Piki must be white, yellow, blue, and red. He tell boy to take to mountain near village and scatter bread before he go home.

"The wife of the boy, she get fat with child. Long way back to village. Boy scatter piki in right way on mountain, white, yellow, red, and blue. The mountains all changed quick. This is the way the Hopi people use the color in the mountains. Hopi use red for painting pottery, the red and yellow to paint moccasins, the blue for painting their bodies."

Brad had noticed the different colored bands in the mountains, mesas, and buttes of the southwest when he had journeyed to the Rockies from Missouri.

Gray Owl finished his food, burped loudly, then resumed the telling of the Snake Dance story.

"The boy and his woman come to the mountain where Hopi village sits on top of mesa. Woman tells boy to climb up. She will wait at bottom. The boy climbs to top of mesa, to village. People ask him about the Lower World. He say to give him a kiva, and he build fire, tell story. Story take all night to tell. Boy tells his journey to all the people.

"In morning, boy walks down to take wife some food. On his way, he meet woman carrying jar of water. She walks back up the mountain. Boy knows this woman. She was in his blankets when he was younger. She puts her arms around him. He walks down and wife knows about other woman. She has the tears in her eyes. She says she will go home but leave him their child. She changes into a snake after her son sees light and goes back to her home. Son lives with father, but he is part snake. That is why the Hopi dance the Snake Dance: to honor that snake son and bring good things to the people."

Brad let out a breath.

"That's a hell of a story, Gray Owl," he said, then asked, "So, why do you come here? This is Ute and Arapaho country. Did you run out of snakes where you live?"

"No, I bring sidewinder to Wading Crow. My people join with his people. Hopi say little snake boy come to Arapaho when he grew to a man. I find Wading Crow and tell him story. He say his people talk about Snake Dance. He want me to teach Arapaho people. We catch snakes. We go to his village. I teach Snake Dance."

"And I killed the sidewinder," Brad said. "Does that wreck your Snake Dance?"

He finished eating and handed the empty bowl back to Gray Owl. Gray Owl set it next to his.

"I do not know. Maybe you come to Snake Dance. You have snake spirit now."

"Where is this Arapaho village?" Brad asked.

"Many sleeps from this place. High in mountains. Place like Hopi mesa. Big, long, flat mountain."

"Maybe a butte," Brad said, but Gray Owl did not know the word.

"I do not know," he said. "Big, long, flat mountain."

"A butte, we call it in English."

"It is good place. Strong with good spirits. You come. We make the Snake Dance."

"I can't, Gray Owl. I have a little ranch to run. I raise cattle."

"Ah, that is good. Much food."

"Yes," Brad said. He flexed his left hand slightly, just to see if it still worked. There was only a little pain, more like stings where Gray Owl had made the cuts. He looked at it and saw that it was only slightly swollen. The food felt good in his stomach. He stood up and asked Gray Owl for water. Gray Owl gave him an earthen vessel. Brad brought it to his lips, tipped it, and drank.

"Good, good," Gray Owl said. "You drink. Make blood pure."

"I hope you're right. Thank you for saving my life."

"No save Sidewinder's life. The Great Spirit watches you. He gives favor. Maybe you now Snake Man."

Brad laughed, but he felt uncomfortable. He didn't believe in spirits, and he did not know the Hopi or the Arapaho people. They had their ways, and he had his. It was odd that a Hopi would come to Colorado and live with the Arapaho. He thought all Indians were on reservations. Maybe this tribe had escaped the army's roundup and were hiding out. As long as they weren't attacking settlers, taking scalps, their secret was safe with him.

But now, after thinking about the story Gray Owl had told him, he wondered if Gray Owl didn't have a hidden purpose in telling him that story. And he had invited him to join in the Snake Dance. That just didn't sound right to him.

Visions of human sacrifice sprung up in Brad's mind. He wondered if he went to the Arapaho village, if they would kill him because he had killed the snake that Gray Owl had brought from his Hopi tribe's village. He looked at the Hopi as if he could read the man's mind by his actions. Gray Owl was paying no attention to him and seemed as normal as any man, red or white.

"Storm's coming," Brad said to Gray Owl as he stepped outside and saw the clouds building in the sky.

"Much rain," Gray Owl said.

The Hopi seemed to taste the air as he gazed upward at the sky. In the distance, both men heard the faint rumblings of thunder, and when they looked to the north, they could see the elephantine undersides of dark thunderclouds.

"Heap rain," Gray Owl said again, his tongue flicking over his lips as if he had tasted the coming rain.

An hour later, when Brad was dozing on a buffalo robe inside the shelter, he heard the whicker of a horse. He knew that the Indians had no horses with them. Gray Owl told him they had walked from the far butte somewhere deep in the mountains. He sat up and saw that Gray Owl was already outside, and the sky had darkened considerably. In a few minutes, the sun would be blotted out. As he got to his feet, he heard the sound of thunder again, closer this time, and he thought he saw a flicker of light in the distant sky, silver light, quick and elusive, as bright as quicksilver.

He walked outside.

"Wading Crow come," Gray Owl said. "And two others. Three horses."

Brad's heart quickened.

"I don't see them," he said.

"Listen. They come soon."

Brad listened. He heard dry tree branch crunch and a crackle of leaves, the ring of a horseshoe on stone. What? Half a mile? Quarter of a mile? Close, but he knew that sound carried far in the thin air of the mountains. They were at a higher elevation than his ranch, he knew, but not even close to timberline.

Then he saw Wading Crow. The Arapaho was riding Ginger. And behind him, two more riders. He saw a flash of shiny burgundy and knew that was Julio's horse, Chato.

He could not see the other rider clearly, but his heart was racing.

"Woman come," Gray Owl said softly.

"I can't see her."

"Wait. You see."

And he did a few seconds later. His heart soared as he

recognized Felicity. Just the jaunty angle of her hat and the way she sat her saddle told him that she was there, with Julio and Wading Crow. His throat tightened as he felt a rush of emotion.

He raised his right arm to wave.

Then the dark clouds hid the sun and it grew dark. The wind rose in high gusts, streaming powerful jets across the ridge. The shelter shook and rattled like a giant bird ruffling its feathers.

And there, on top of Wading Crow's head, was his hat. Brad's eyes shone at the sight. Involuntarily he touched his hand to his head. It felt naked and was still tender. He smiled.

A damned hat, he thought.

Not my horse or my wife but my damned hat.

And he felt very rich at that moment, as if he owned all the treasures of the world.

Felicity waved, and something melted inside his chest. His knees turned to jelly, and his insides quivered and warmed.

He waved back and choked up, unable to speak.

Gray Owl looked at him and smiled.

"Your heart soars," Gray Owl said, and that was all.

It was enough.

And, it was true.

NINE

❧

Pilar gasped in horror as she watched Cholo chase his own tail, his foamy jaws snapping, teeth clacking. The dog was growling and howling at the same time.

"*Loco perro*," she shouted and grabbed her broom from beside the door. She ran outside, chasing Cholo, shouting and screaming, her calico skirt whipping about her legs, her sandals flopping with each leaping step.

The dog saw Pilar and snarled at her, shrinking away like a shadow retreating under the sun.

"Cholo," she said, in Spanish, "what passes with you? Are you sick?"

The dog snarled and charged at Pilar. She swung the broom and batted Cholo in the head. The dog yelped and cringed once again, glaring at her with feverish eyes.

Frightened now, Pilar called out.

"Carlos. Carlos. Come quick. The dog is crazy."

Carlos was behind his bunkhouse at the well, staring down at two other dogs, Pepe and Pelon. Pelon was already dead, and Pepe was dying, writhing next to the well, his yellowish coat filled with briars and all matted up from wallowing in mud down by the creek. He heard Pilar's call and backed away from Pepe. He ran down in front of the other bunkhouse, which Pilar had made into a fairly large and comfortable house with a Franklin cookstove, curtains, chairs, a bedroom with a large bed, and a large, comfortable living room. They still called it "the bunkhouse," but it was that no longer.

Carlos had his hand on his pistol grip, ready to draw it from his holster when he heard Pilar call his name.

"It is Cholo," Pilar cried, pointing to the dog, who was now crouched and snarling at her, foam flecking its mouth as if it had dipped into Julio's shaving mug.

"Stay away from Cholo, Pilar," he said, waving his arms. "He is sick."

Then, to Pilar's surprise, Carlos ran up to Cholo and drew his six-gun. He aimed it at the dog's head and pulled the trigger. The explosion was deafening. Orange sparks and smoke belched from the Remington's snout. The bullet struck Cholo in his jaw, blew out his brains. Teeth and tongue flew away like meat scraps, and brain matter plowed into the ground like cast-off bits of pudding.

Pilar screamed and covered her face.

Cholo stiffened and was still.

"I have another one, Pilar. Wait here."

She took her hands away from her face and stared at Carlos without comprehension. He ran back to the well, and she turned her back on the dead dog after one last quick look.

She heard the pistol shot and jumped at the report. It seemed to her that she jumped inside her skin. She slowly walked back to the bunkhouse she had converted into a home for her and Julio, stood next to the door, looking down at the flowers growing in empty Arbuckles coffee tins. Pansies and petunias, red and white gardenias, buttercups, and morning glories. By the time Carlos returned, she was trembling, her hands shaking uncontrollably.

"What did you do, Carlos?"

"Pepe was suffering. Pelon was already dead."

"All the dogs? All three?"

"Yes. The hydrophobia."

"Ah. Poisoned," she said.

"Yes. It is a bad way to die. I will bury the dogs."

"Who could have done such a thing?" She asked, her voice a querulous spiral that rose to an almost hysterical pitch.

"Bad men," he said. "Did not Julio tell you about the horse tracks down near the creek?"

"No. He said nothing."

"Well, maybe he did not want to worry you."

"What about the horse tracks?"

"It is nothing. Riders passing by, perhaps."

"It is more than that, Carlos." She had stopped shaking now that she had a new worry to make her fret.

"Maybe," he said. "I go now. I must clean my pistol and put more bullets in the cylinder."

"You are worried, is it not so?" she said.

"Worried? About what?"

"Those men. Maybe they are the ones who—who poisoned the dogs."

"I do not know."

She grabbed Carlos by the shoulder and whirled him around to face her.

"You do know," she said. "Men on horseback. Passing by? Men do not pass by without speaking. Unless they are . . ." She paused, searching for the word. "Spying," she finished.

"Maybe they rode by at night when we were all sleeping, so they did not stop and give a greeting. Who knows?"

She glared at him but softened her gaze. Carlos was not at fault. He had done nothing. But she wondered why Julio had not told her about the men, the tracks of the horses. He was the one she should have anger for, her own husband. Keeping secrets. Oh, she could shake him for not telling her.

Well, she thought, she would have much to say to Julio when he returned.

"Go and bury the dogs, Carlos," she said. "Clean your pistol. Put fresh cartridges in it. Bury them deep and put stones on their graves or the wolves will feast on them."

"I will do this, Pilar."

He touched a finger to the brim of his hat and headed for his own bunkhouse. He would get a shovel from the barn and bury the dogs up in the timber where the ground was not so rocky. He would bury them deep and cover them with stones.

Then, he would ride around the valley looking for horse tracks. He would look, too, for the meat that was contaminated with strychnine.

That was a horrible way for a dog to die.

Or a man.

TEN

❧

Felicity squealed with delight when Brad rushed up to her, helped her dismount. She flung her arms around him, squeezed him tight with both arms. She sniffed his manly scent, and her legs crumpled as her knees turned to gelatin. He surrounded her with his own arms and kept her from sliding to the ground.

"Oh, Brad," she breathed, "I'm so glad to see you, to see you all in one piece."

"What did you expect?" he chided, smoothing her hair with one hand, tilting her hat back on one side.

"I—I didn't," she said, suddenly at a loss for words, her brain muddled with a half dozen images, her emotions rushing up in a tangle of senses. The feel of his warm body, the strong scent of him, the reassuring flex of his muscled arms around her. She wanted never to leave him, never to let him out of her sight again.

Wading Crow dismounted, grabbed the leather bag with the timber rattler in it, and handed it to Gray Owl. He took out the forked stick and tossed it beside the shelter. Then he took off Brad's hat and carried it to him.

Brad broke his embrace and took the hat, looked it over.

"Thanks," he said. "And for my horse, too, Wading Crow. And thanks for bringing my wife and Julio up here."

"*De nada*," Wading Crow said.

Brad reshaped his hat slightly and put it on.

"You were hurt," Felicity said.

"A little."

"I saw blood on your hat."

"That blood was from the rock that fell on me," he said. "Don't you recognize rock blood when you see it, darlin'?"

Felicity laughed, but she wanted to take him in her arms again and check the top of his head. Then she saw his left hand and gasped.

"Did the rock fall on your hand?" she said.

He held it up so that they both could look at it.

"Snake nipped me," he said. "Gray Owl over there cut me and sucked most of the poison out. Hand'll be good as new in two shakes of a lamb's tail."

"Oh, you," she said. "Getting hurt doesn't mean much to you, Brad."

"Not much."

"Well, it does to me."

"Want me to tie up the horses, Brad?" Julio asked. "Do we ride back to the rancho now? The sky is already getting dark. There will be much rain soon."

Brad could see that Julio was nervous. He kept glancing toward the two Indians and a muscle in his cheek twitched.

"Find a dry place to tie them up, Julio. Under some big trees, maybe. Unsaddle them and break out the slickers. We'll be here awhile. I owe these two men my life. It wouldn't be good to rush off."

He looked up at the darkening sky. The sun was barely visible now, shielded by thin scrims of clouds that were racing east but being overtaken by the big clouds, some of which were turning as black as anthracite coal.

Julio nodded. He grabbed the reins of Felicity's horse,

Rose, then caught up Ginger's reins and headed into the timber.

"Come," Wading Crow said, gesturing to Brad and Felicity. "Rain soon."

Felicity stopped just outside the shelter, looking up at the top and sides. The shelter was really two lean-tos with a double beam at the top. The Indians had cut small thick spruce trees, trimmed the bottoms, and cut a single branch to make a kind of hook. The hooks were set over each beam and more small spruces were set in the trough between them on small cross-beam supports. There were trimmed tree branches crisscrossed on both sides of the sloping roof, and these, too, had small, hooked spruce trees draping them, so that all of the trees overlapped and offered shelter from the rain and wind.

"This is very nicely built," Felicity said. "You could almost live in it."

When she stepped inside, she saw Gray Owl drop the snake out of its bag into a basket. Then she heard all the snakes rattling, and she shrank back against Brad for protection.

"Wait until you see Gray Owl feed them mice and rats," he said.

Felicity shuddered. Brad put an arm around her.

He took off her hat and stroked her hair. He had the right touch. She began to relax.

"Gray Owl, this is my wife," Brad said in Spanish. "She is called *Felicidad*, Felicity, in English."

"With much pleasure," Gray Owl said in Spanish. "Sit. Do you have hunger?"

"I have a little hunger," she replied in the same tongue. Then, in English, "Brad, I brought sandwiches for the three of us. But we can share with Gray Owl and Walking Crow."

"What is sandwich?" Walking Crow asked.

"You will see," Brad said.

Brad put their hats near the door. He and Felicity sat on a buffalo robe.

"This is where I slept last night," he told her. "Snug as a bug in a rug."

She rubbed her fingers in the deep fur of the buffalo robe.

"Nice," she said, and glanced around at all the baskets. She heard hissing and rattles, and she snuggled close to Brad.

"Can they get out?" she whispered to him.

"Not unless you open a basket and call to them," he said. "They'll come a-runnin' if you do that, like trained pups."

"Don't joke about a thing like that," she said.

"You need to stop thinking about those snakes, darlin'."

"How can I?"

Brad smiled. He was thinking about the snakes, too. After all, one of them, a sidewinder, had gotten out, and it had sunk its fangs into his hand. He winced at the thought.

In a few minutes Julio returned, carrying saddlebags, three rifles, and three canteens.

He set them down just inside the shelter, next to Felicity's and Brad's hats.

He handed two yellow slickers to Brad and kept one for himself.

"I put the saddles and bridles under a deadfall," he said. "Covered them up good with branches and leaves. We should ride back to the rancho, I think."

Julio eyed the Hopi and the Arapaho as if they were poisonous snakes, ready to strike at any minute.

"Sit yourself, Julio," Brad said in Spanish. "We will eat soon and wait out the rain. Maybe it will blow over quick."

Brad knew that storms in the mountains were unpredictable. They could come up suddenly and blow on by just as quickly. Or, at certain times, they could rage for days, not with just one lone storm but a passel of them, streaming down from the north, one after the other. It was early spring in the Rockies, and this might be just one of those spring storms that lasted only an hour or two.

"We can't stay the night, Brad," Felicity said. "We can eat on the ride back."

"There's no hurry, is there?" He thought he had detected an odd tone in Felicity's voice, as if there was more to her thoughts than what she was saying.

"I—I don't know," she said. "Maybe."

"The brindle cow, she come back," Julio said, and Brad saw a look pass between him and Felicity.

"She did?" Brad said. "When?"

"This morning, as we were leaving," Felicity said.

Again, there was a sharp look between his wife and Julio.

"So, we can go back, eh?" Julio said. "Maybe we can ride faster than the storm."

As if in answer, there was a flash of light inside the shelter. Five seconds later, they heard a loud rumble of the thunder. There was more thunder right behind it, sounding like an empty warehouse full of rolling barrels.

Brad had been counting the seconds between the lightning and the thunder. Five seconds.

"That was about five miles away," he said. "We can't beat it, and if we ride out there, we're liable to get fried to a crisp by a lightning strike."

Wading Crow walked over to the three sitting by the entrance.

"No good ride," he said. "Big storm. Much rain. Lightning kill like bullet. You stay."

"But . . ." Felicity started to say, but the look on Brad's face told her she might want to keep quiet. She knew that look, as a wife knows her husband's ways.

"We will accept your hospitality, Wading Crow," she said, and Brad smiled at her, a quick smile that told her she had done the right thing.

"Heap food. Many robes. Plenty wood make fire. Fire make warm. Sleep good," Wading Crow said, and walked away.

"I never knew Indians could be so polite," she whispered. "Well, I guess we'll stay then. After all, we're not at war with them. I don't expect they'll scalp us."

"Indians learned scalping from the white man, Felicity. And probably some of our other bad habits as well."

"Oh, you're just making that up," she said in a playful voice, then slapped a hand on his chest. She jerked her hand back right away and a startled look flared the light in her eyes.

"What was that?" she said.

"What?"

"When I hit you just then, I felt something. Have you got a bug or a spider on your chest?"

Brad looked down and patted his chest. He had forgotten about the rattles. He had tucked the lanyard inside his shirt and just forgotten about it.

He pulled on the thin sinew and drew out the set of rattles. He shook them in Felicity's face, and she drew back in shock.

"Oooh," she said, "get it away from me."

She scooted away from him a few inches. He continued to shake the rattles and dangled them still closer.

"It won't bite," Brad said.

"That's cruel, Brad. You know I'm scared of snakes."

He stopped shaking the rattles and slipped them back inside his shirt.

"Gray Owl cut these off the snake that bit me," he said.

Felicity's eyes widened.

"Oh," she said. "Are you going to keep them?"

"Sure."

"Well, I hope you're not going to wear them."

"Well, they're not much good in a drawer at home."

"Brad, you aren't going to wear them around me, you hear?"

"Certainly not, darlin'. Those rattles would give you too much warning."

"What?"

"Well, sometimes a man likes to sneak up on a woman."

"Oh, you. That's not funny."

"It's funny to me." He turned and looked at Julio. "Isn't it funny to you, Julio?"

"It is a little funny," Julio admitted, but his heart wasn't in it. The last thing he wanted to do was get into the middle of an argument between a man and his wife. He pulled his legs up and rested both arms on them, as if he was a turtle drawing into its shell.

"See, Felicity? Julio thinks it's funny."

"You know what I mean," she said.

"I'll keep the rattles as a souvenir," he said.

"In a drawer. In the tack room. Out in the barn."

"Whatever you say, darlin'."

And she knew he wasn't going to obey her wishes. But she would never let him wear them when they were in bed together. That was a sacred place to her and no place for souvenir rattlesnake rattles. And she knew he would abide by that particular ruling. She scooted back toward him, a sly, coy look on her face.

The shelter lit up with a flash of lightning, and two seconds later a peal of thunder rolled across the skies. The thunder shook the shelter and the ground beneath them.

"Close," Brad said.

Then they all raised their heads and listened to the first spatters of rain hitting the trees outside and tinking on the spruce boughs. Moments later, the wind picked up, blowing rain inside the hut, lashing the cut boughs, and wailing high in the trees.

Felicity nestled against Brad. He put his arms around her.

"I'm so glad we're not out there in this," she said.

In counterpoint to the rain, some of the rattlesnakes, disturbed, began to clatter. Brad felt Felicity shiver against him as a crack of lightning struck within a few yards of the shelter.

Brad could smell the ozone, taste it like copper in his mouth.

He, too, was glad that they were not riding through this storm, out in the open where the lightning danced across the land like an electric lattice.

And the darkness steeped around them while Gray Owl

scratched his flint on steel to start the fire. A thousand tom-toms and kettle drums boomed outside, and the rain blew straight and hard, shooting silvery lances through the openings in the spruce boughs.

ELEVEN

❧

The wind howled through the trees, cracking limbs, hurtling pine branches to the ground with loud crashes. To those in the makeshift shelter, it sounded like cannon and gunfire, as if armies were clashing in mortal combat all around them. The sky was so dark, it felt like night, and the flashes of lightning only served to heighten the illusion of a great war in the mountains.

The rattling of the snakes inside the baskets reached a feverish pitch, adding to the din. Then the hail fell from the sky and, blown by the wind, sounded like grapeshot striking the trees, both living and dead, littering the ground with white pellets. A few entered the shelter, stung Julio's back and arms until he moved away from the entrance, and a couple hit the fire, hissed, and melted in almost the twinkling of an eye.

The five people munched on fresh beef sandwiches, packed with mustard, ketchup, and boiled turnip greens. Gray Owl kept the fire bright with fresh wood, and shadows danced to the tune of the hail and rain.

Julio moved closer to the fire, sitting near Felicity and
Brad on the buffalo robe. They drank water from their
canteens. The men stepped outside to relieve themselves
until Felicity could stand it no longer. She donned her
slicker and ventured outside, too, after the hail stopped.
Brad went with her. When she found a place, he took off
his slicker and held it over her as she squatted next to the
south side of a large juniper tree. They both heard the horses
whinny several yards away.

When she had finished, Brad said, "Let's check on the
horses before we go back."

"Good idea," she said, her face glistening with rain
drops.

The horses were packed together, their rumps to the
wind. All wore the long rope halters Brad always carried
with him when he rode off the ranch. He sometimes let
the horses graze while he and Julio had lunch. He couldn't
find the saddles and bridles. It was too dark. He patted the
necks of each horse and spoke soothingly to them.

"I'm glad I left Curly inside when I left," Felicity said.
"But, he's going to be scared."

"Yeah. Curly doesn't like storms."

"He doesn't like thunder and lightning, you mean."

"I know he shakes like he's passing peach seeds every
time a storm comes up."

"Runs under our bed and hides."

"Is that a safe place?" Brad kidded. "It's good to know."

"Not for you it isn't," she said, and they ducked their
heads and trotted back through the trees. They could see
the soft glow of firelight inside the Indian hut. They had
forgotten to wear their hats, which probably saved those
from being blown away, and when they returned, their heads
were soaked to the scalp. They looked like a pair of drowned
rats, but no one in the shelter laughed at them.

Felicity shook out her hair and combed it with her fingers, letting the warm air from the fire blow through her
tresses until they dried.

The darkness came on, and the wind died down. But the rain persisted, and sometimes a gust would spray water through the small openings and spatter the fire and the people sitting around it, looking for all the world like a gathering of ascetics on some dark pilgrimage to the nether regions.

Gray Owl lit a small clay pipe and offered it around. Julio and Brad both shook their heads.

"You do not take the smoke?" Gray Owl said to Brad.

"Too hard to get tobacco. We live a long way from a general store."

"Tobacco is good. To smoke is good."

Brad noticed that Gray Owl had sprinkled some of the tobacco into the fire before he packed his pipe. And then he had blown smoke to the four directions before offering it to the others. Wading Crow took the pipe and did the same thing, blowing smoke in four directions.

"The Mexican sheepherders who bring their sheep to the mountains in summer bring much tobacco. We buy, we trade." Wading Crow passed the pipe back to Gray Owl. "We have much tobacco. We buy the old sheep from them."

"Wading Crow does not like sheep much," Gray Owl remarked. "He likes the beef."

"But we do not have beef anymore. If you have beef, Sidewinder, I would like to buy some cows from you."

"I have beef," Brad said. "I suppose I could sell you a few head. How will you pay?"

"I will pay in gold."

"Gold?"

"My people have much gold."

Julio's eyebrows arched in surprise.

"Dust or nuggets?" Brad asked.

"Some dust. Some small nuggets. We have a scale as well."

"Do you know where my ranch is?" Brad asked.

"Do you not live in the valley below where the Mexicano Albert once lived?"

Brad exchanged a look with Julio. Felicity looked puzzled. She wore a quizzical expression on her face.

"Who is this Albert?" she asked. "Why have I never heard of him?"

"Julio, did you show her the burned house?" Brad asked.

"Yes. I did not tell her who had once lived there."

"That was Albert's house? Who was he? What happened?"

"Seguin," Wading Crow said. "Albert Seguin. He and his woman, his two sons were killed by a very bad man, a stealer of cattle. There was an American boy living with him also. He, too, was killed. I did not know his name. He said he had run away."

"He was from Denver, I heard," Julio said. "The white boy. I had forgotten about him. His father rode down from Denver, took his body back there to be buried."

"Do you know who the rustlers were?" Brad asked.

Gray Owl passed the pipe back to Wading Crow. He puffed slowly on it.

"We know the stealers of cattle," he said. "Two brothers. They are called Coombs. The leader is Delbert. His brother is called Hiram. They are very bad white men. They are much feared."

Brad looked at Julio.

"I did not know who the rustlers were. I did not want to know. I did not ask."

"How horrible," Felicity said. "To murder those poor people over a few head of cattle."

"The bad men live in Oro City," Wading Crow said. "They steal from good men."

"What do they do with the cattle they steal?" Brad asked.

"They are what you call butchers," Wading Crow said. "They sell the meat to those who cook and sell food in the towns."

"Why hasn't somebody stopped them?" Felicity asked. "Why doesn't the law arrest them?"

"I do not know," Wading Crow said.

"Julio?" Brad looked straight at him.

"I think people are afraid. And it is said that they pay the town marshal and the sheriff. There is much money to be made in selling cattle that cost no pesos to the thieves."

"Damn," Brad said. "Somebody ought to do something. Back in Missouri, they would be hanged."

"They do not hang such men in Oro City," Julio said glumly.

They all sat silent for a time, listening to the soft patter of rain on the spruce-laden shelter. Felicity wondered if she ought to tell Brad about the horse tracks down by the creek. She could not help thinking about them now, especially after learning about the Seguin family. Maybe the Coombs brothers were scouting out their ranch, counting heads, with an idea to rustle their entire herd, some two hundred cows. No, now was not that time. They were stuck up here in the storm. She would tell him on the way back or wait until they got home.

"Wading Crow," Felicity said, after a time, "why did you call my husband 'Sidewinder'? His name is Brad. Brad Storm."

"Indian name, Sidewinder."

She looked at Brad. "Your Indian name? When did this happen?"

"This morning, I think. Last night maybe. It's just what they call me."

"Him good medicine," Gray Owl said. "Strong medicine. Kill sidewinder." He made a rattling sound with his teeth.

Wading Crow had been thinking. He was counting on his fingers. Brad watched him, wondered what he was figuring in that Arapaho brain of his.

"Sidewinder," Wading Crow said, "you bring ten cow. I give two ounces for cow."

"Two ounces of gold for each cow?" Brad said.

Wading Crow nodded. "Ten cow. Twenty ounce. You bring. I make map to village."

Brad looked at Felicity, who seemed lost.

"That's more than we could get in Pueblo," Brad said. "More than we could in Denver. Even if we drove them to the railhead in Kansas, we probably wouldn't get that much."

"How much is it in greenbacks?" she asked.

"Thirty-two dollars a head, Felicity. Three hundred and twenty dollars for ten cows."

She let out a low whistle.

"I could buy you that dress you wanted in Oro City," he said. "The one at Cotter's store."

"Oh, Brad. That was just a-wishin'."

"Well, wishes do come true sometimes, you know."

He looked at Wading Crow.

"When do you want the cattle?"

"Seven sleeps."

"That's a week, darlin'."

"I make good map," Wading Crow said. "You come. Do Snake Dance."

"Whoa," Brad said. "I'm not . . ."

"What's he talking about, Brad? Dance with snakes?"

"Never mind, honey. He's just joking."

"No joke," Gray Owl said. "Sidewinder make good Snake Dance. Bring good luck."

"Wading Crow, I'll bring the cattle to you in a week, but I want no part of your Snake Dance. If that particular string is attached, I won't bring the cattle."

"You bring. I pay."

"But no Snake Dance. Right?"

Wading Crow smiled. He waved a hand in the air as if to dismiss the very idea of a Snake Dance.

Brad wasn't so sure.

"Don't you go anywhere near those snakes, Brad," Felicity said.

Julio looked sick. As if he had been kicked in the stomach.

The snakes had stopped rattling.

But Julio could still hear them, and the two Indians made

him nervous. He told himself he would stay awake all night, just in case. With one hand on his pistol. The other on his rifle.

"Good," Gray Owl said, finishing up his small clay pipe. It was pink, made from pipestone, traded long years before from a Southern Cheyenne. It was a good pipe. "Make sleep now. Much rain all night."

Felicity wrapped her arms around Brad's arms and yawned.

"I am tired," she said. "Let's get some sleep."

"Yeah." He was still thinking about the Snake Dance and the cattle and the gold. They could use the money. From what Wading Crow said, it would be a fairly long trip. Three or four days if they didn't have to climb any big mountains.

He would work all that out with Wading Crow in the morning, he thought. He helped Felicity make up their bed. They pulled the buffalo robe over them.

Gray Owl added more wood to the fire and spoke to Julio.

"You sleep," he said. "No worry."

Julio's eyes widened.

Did the Indian read his thoughts? Gray Owl showed him a place to sleep on a deerskin he had unrolled.

Julio could not refuse. He dared not refuse.

He still didn't trust either Gray Owl or Wading Crow, but he had much tiredness and his eyelids were as heavy as lead sash weights. He lay down on the skin, but he didn't carry his rifle over to the bed. He took his pistol belt off and loosened the pistol in its holster. He kept one hand on the butt as he closed his eyes.

Brad took one last look at the smoke hole. There were no stars, no moon. Only blackness and the silvery streaks of rain flashing past the opening.

Almost as good as stars, he thought, as Felicity draped an arm over his chest and snuggled close to him. The smell of her hair and the silkiness of it was the last thing he remembered that night.

TWELVE

❧

Two hours before dawn, the patter of rain diminished to whispers by the time the eastern horizon cracked open a rent in the sky. There was only a mist in the high trees, a thin blanket of fog in the low-lying valleys. The jays circled the encampment, squawking and chattering, while the squirrels and chipmunks ventured forth, sipping water from the leaves, gnawing on pine nuts.

Brad cocked one eye open, focused on the smoke hole. He saw a paling sky, heard movement a few feet away. He opened the other eye and looked down at Felicity. She was still sound asleep, her lips parted invitingly, her face serene. He looked across the shelter and saw Gray Owl holding a mouse by the tail. He dropped it into a basket, and Brad heard the whirring sound of a rattlesnake. There was a swishing sound in the basket, a tiny squeak, and then the rattles were still.

Wading Crow was nowhere in sight.

Julio was still asleep, his pistol on his chest, both hands clutching it as if it were a child's stuffed toy. Brad smiled. Julio might never get over his fear and mistrust of Indians.

Brad wondered what Gray Owl and Wading Crow thought of the Mexican and his obvious fear that he would be scalped in his sleep or his throat would be cut open like a sliced melon.

Brad slid from under the blanket, very carefully, so he would not disturb Felicity. He stepped over to Gray Owl and talked to him in sign, asking him where Wading Crow was. He had learned some of the sign from an old Lakota drover in Denver who helped him drive his first herd up to Oro City and into the mountains where he had bought his ranch.

Gray Owl cupped a hand to his ear and pointed to a direction outside the shelter. Brad nodded that he understood, and walked outside and into the dripping pine trees. He heard the noises more distinctly now and walked toward them.

Wading Crow was putting fresh lashes on a large travois he had resurrected from the forest floor, two long poles, stripped of bark, tied securely together at one end, leaving a large, wide V between their loose ends.

"What are you doing?" Brad asked.

"Seven suns, we go."

"Do you and Gray Owl pull that travvy by yourselves all through the mountains to your village?"

"Make smoke. Friends come. Bring horses."

"Smoke signals?"

Wading Crow pointed through the trees.

"Big hill. Make fire. Green wood. Make smoke. Village see. Bring horses. Bring braves. Pull travois. Take snakes to village."

"I understand," Brad said. "You were going to make me a map."

"Wading Crow make map," he said, and leaned the tied end of the travois against the trunk of a tall pine tree.

Brad wondered if he was going to use an animal skin to draw the map, the underside of a rabbit skin or a patch of deerskin, perhaps. Instead, Wading Crow walked over to a dry spot beneath a tree, scuffed away the pine needles until he had a patch of bare earth about two or three feet in circumference. He drew his knife from its scabbard. He cut a small branch from beneath a spruce tree, skinned it down to a bare stick. He sharpened one end to a point. Then he knelt down before the bare patch and, with the pointed end of the stick, drew a crude map. For their present position, he drew an inverted *V*. Then he drew a line and on either side he inscribed landmarks, ridges, passes. At the other end he drew a number of inverted *V*s to represent the Arapaho village.

"Three sleeps walk. Six sleeps drive cattle."

"Six days," Brad murmured. "Just follow the valleys and low ridges."

Walking Crow nodded. "No big mountain on trail."

"You want me to remember all this? I thought you were going to give me a map I could hold in my hand."

"Secret village. No map in hand. Only here." He tapped a finger to his temple, indicating that Brad should memorize the map.

"You don't want people, white men, to know where your village is?"

"No. White man take red man to camp. Big camp. Make red man slave."

"A reservation?"

"Big camp. No game. No fish. Bad place."

Brad knew that a number of Indian tribes had been moved to so-called reservations, given a house, a hoe, and maybe a mule. Trouble was most of the places were where no white man would or could live. The Indians could not grow crops. They could not hunt or fish, and were entirely dependent on the white man for subsistence. So Wading Crow and his people must have been hiding out from white men for some time. He wondered how they survived the brutal winters in the Rocky Mountains.

Brad studied the crude map. Then Wading Crow took the stick and drew a large *X* on his dirt map and then a small scraggly line to another place where he put an even larger *X*. Then he drew a line from the big *X* to the path he had marked for Brad to follow when he drove the ten head of cattle to the Arapaho village.

Wading Crow pointed at the little *X*. "Albert," he said. Then he jabbed a finger into the center of the large *X*. "This Sidewinder."

Brad saw it all then, the Albert Seguin place where his cows had wandered, his own ranch, and a way to drive his cattle without coming back up the mountain to where the Arapaho and the Hopi had built their hunting camp.

"Good," Brad said. "How did you know where my ranch was?"

"Me know. Me know heap."

"You've seen my property?"

"Hunt long ago. Hunt deer. Kill many."

"What about Seguin? Albert? Did you know him well."

"Albert good friend."

"I hope I can be your friend, Wading Crow."

The Arapaho smiled.

He dropped the stick and gave Brad a hug.

"You good friend, Sidewinder."

Wading Crow obliterated his map with the sole of his moccasin, kicked pine needles and dirt over the spot.

"Deer scrape," he said.

Brad laughed. Then Wading Crow opened his fly and urinated on the spot.

"Deer scrape," Brad said, and Wading Crow chuckled.

They walked back to the shelter together. Julio was digging out the saddles and bridles.

"I did not bring oats or corn for the horses," he said. "Do we go home now?"

"Yes," Brad said. "I'll help you saddle up, Julio, after I awaken Felicity."

"She is awake. She talks to Gray Owl."

"I see you and your pistol survived the night," Brad said.

Julio's face twisted and collapsed in puzzlement. But Wading Crow got the joke, and he grunted what might be taken as a chuckle in his society.

"Never mind," Brad said, and walked off with Wading Crow.

Gray Owl was teaching Felicity how to make sign. He showed her a man on horseback, and Felicity was delighted. Gray Owl made the sign for sun and water and mountains.

"Brad, why haven't you taught me to speak in sign language?"

"I don't know. Never thought of it I guess."

"I know you learned from Red Bonnet, that Oglala drover you hired."

"Some, yes."

"I guess I was too busy being a cook when we came up here."

"It's not something you use all the time," he said.

"But, it's a wonderful way to talk."

"Maybe more women should learn sign," he said, and instantly regretted it.

"You mean you want women to keep their mouths shut?"

Brad held up both hands in surrender.

"I didn't say that," he said.

"That's what you meant."

"I'm sorry. It was a slip of the tongue."

"At least now I know how you really feel about women," she said.

"Whoa, Felicity. That's not how I feel about women. Have I ever clamped a hand over your mouth to shut you up?"

"No, but you've told me to shut up often enough."

"Only when I was losing an argument with you," he said.

Felicity smiled.

"You're forgiven," she said, and jumped to her feet, wrapped both arms around him, and peppered his neck with kisses on both sides.

Brad's face turned the color of a ripe peach as he pushed her away.

"Enough of that," he said. "I'm going to help Julio saddle up. We're riding back home."

"I almost hate to leave," she said.

"I'm going to pick out some good cattle for Wading Crow when we get back. Then Julio and I will drive them to his village."

"So soon?"

"Probably leave in a week. Take us better'n a week to drive them there and get back."

"I'll miss you," she said.

He waved a hand at her and walked out to help Julio.

They had the horses saddled within ten minutes, then led them back to the hut. Felicity was waiting outside. So, too, were Gray Owl and Wading Crow. Brad shook their hands and said good-bye.

Felicity said good-bye.

Julio just stood there, a blank expression his face.

"Aren't you going to say good-bye, Julio?" Felicity asked.

"*Adios*," he said, begrudgingly, Brad thought.

"*Adios, hermano*," Wading Crow said.

Gray Owl said something in Hopi. Brad took it to mean either "good-bye" or "may the bad spirits take you to the Lower Place."

The three mounted up and turned their horses. Felicity and Brad turned and waved good-bye and got waves in return.

"Julio, you were rude to those Indians. They saved Brad's life."

"I did not mean to be rude," he said.

"So, you don't like Indians."

"No, I do not like them much."

"Those were nice men. Weren't they, Brad?"

"Very nice," he said, hoping Felicity would drop it. She knew better than to argue with one of his hands.

And, to his surprise, Felicity said no more, and as they rode back to the place where the brindle cow had run off from the other cattle, the pain in Brad's hand and the one on his head began to recede. There was sunshine, and the grass gave off a heady scent. The air smelled fresh-scrubbed and there were wildflowers all through the valley, giving off their aromas.

Just before they reached the ranch later that afternoon, Felicity broke her silence.

"Brad, Carlos and Julio found fresh horse tracks down by the creek and up in the timber before we left. Shod horses."

"What?"

"You heard me. Somebody's been watching the place."

"Or counting the cattle," Julio said, eager to be part of the family again.

"Why didn't you tell me this before?" Brad said, too sharply, he knew.

"What good would it have done? There was nothing you could do about it."

"So, why are you telling me now?"

"I just wanted you to know. Oh, dear, I hope all our cattle are still there."

Brad snorted.

"You could have waited all week to say that," he said.

But the worry was on his mind now. After learning about the Seguin family, he didn't feel so secure. He had picked a place far from city life so that he would not have to worry about cattle rustlers and such.

It seemed now that he had not settled far enough away from civilization and the greed of men who preyed on others for their livelihood.

He said nothing, but a feeling of dread began to filter into his senses. And, with the dread, perhaps a small amount of fear.

THIRTEEN

❧

A pair of buzzards circled overhead as Brad, Felicity, and Julio rode toward the Storm house. The buzzards rode the air currents as if they were on wires, wings extended, heads moving from side to side. They were low and flapped their wings only to gain more altitude. But they kept circling.

"Something's dead," Brad said as he pulled on the reins, brought Ginger to a halt.

"*Conejo?*" Julio ventured.

"No, not a rabbit. Something bigger. They'd be on the ground picking a rabbit clean."

Felicity climbed down from Rose, handed the reins to Julio.

"I'm going to let Curly out," she said. "Take care of Rose for me, will you, Julio?"

"And see if you can find Carlos," Brad said, stepping down out of the saddle. He pulled his rifle out of its boot and handed Ginger's reins to Julio.

"I see him," Julio said. "He is down by the creek. He is riding toward us. I will put the horses away."

"Give them each a hatful of grain and a good rubdown, will you?"

"I will do this," Julio said.

Felicity trotted to the house, climbed the porch steps, and opened the front door. Curly romped out and stood on hind legs to lick her face. Felicity laughed and pushed him down. She ran down to greet Brad and jumped up on him, tail wagging furiously. Then the dog ran to the well and lifted a hind leg.

Brad was relieved to see the cattle. They were grazing peacefully. He even saw the brindle cow, alone, separated from the others. She was still the independent spirit among cattle. That would be one he would take to Wading Crow's village, he decided. She had already cost him much. But he had to admit, she had also given him new friends and, perhaps, a different perspective on life. He had felt at home in the Indian camp, oddly serene, in the world but not a part of it. Maybe the brindle was that way herself. There was a good deal to say for the simple life, away from civilization, away from greed and rage, competition and war.

He walked over to the porch and sat on the second step. He watched Carlos on his horse, picking his way across the field, passing through clumps of cattle that seemed indifferent to his presence, all contentedly grazing on good grass. Brad looked up and watched the buzzards dip and glide and swirl on their invisible carousels. The birds were graceful and silent as they sniffed and hunted for carrion.

"*Hola, patrón*," Carlos said as he rode up. "*Qué pasa contigo?*"

"It is a long story," Brad replied in Spanish. "What passes with you?"

"The three dogs they are dead."

"All three? How?"

Carlos described how the dogs had behaved and said that he had to shoot two of them.

"Sounds like strychnine."

"Yes. I think so."

Felicity walked onto the porch and opened the door.

"What's this I hear about the dogs and strychnine?"

"Pilar's dogs are dead," Brad said. "Poisoned, I reckon."

"Oh my god." Then she began calling Curly in a frantic voice. "Curly, here, Curly."

Curly came loping around to the front of the house, ran up on the porch, tail wagging. "You get in this house right away."

She and the dog went into the house.

"Did you find the poisoned meat, Carlos?" Brad asked, getting to his feet.

"No, I do not see the meat anywhere."

"What's this about horse tracks down at the creek and up in the timber?"

Carlos told him what they had seen.

"The tracks wash away in the rain," he said.

"So, no fresh tracks today?"

Carlos shook his head.

"Did it look like someone was scouting out our cattle?"

"I think so," Carlos said. "They sit in the timber for a long time. They do not ride by like travelers."

"We'll have to keep a sharp lookout. I see you're wearing your pistol and have your rifle with you. From now on, we're all going to be armed and ready."

"They will come in the night, I think."

"Why do you think that?"

"I think they watch at night. I do not see riders when the sun is in the sky."

"All right. We'll cross that bridge when we get to it. Keep your eyes peeled."

Felicity went to see Pilar and commiserated with her over the loss of her dogs. They were just curs and Pilar did not take care of them very well, but Felicity knew that she was fond of them and that they provided company for her when Julio was away from the bunkhouse.

During the next few days, Brad selected ten head of cattle that he planned to drive to the Arapaho village. One day, he saw the smoke signals on a peak near the Indian camp and knew that Wading Crow had gotten his thirty snakes and was calling in tribesmen to carry the baskets back to his village. He hated to leave Felicity at such a time, but he had no choice, he thought. He had ridden a wide circle every night, below the creek and up in the timber, watching and listening for horses. Carlos and Julio had done their parts, too, taking turns watching for night riders.

Perhaps, Brad thought, the riders were just curious and were only hunters or travelers. It was hard to figure. While it looked suspicious, he had no proof that rustlers were interested in his herd. Still, the story of the Seguins bothered him, and what he had learned about the Coombs brothers was disturbing.

He and Carlos installed a windmill and pump next to one of the tanks over by the bluffs and the small canyons that lead off the valley. The canyon was full of limestone caves where he would winter his stock. In fact he had done that with a few head the previous winter. Brad's ranch, which he and Felicity had not yet named, was long and wide, with high ground to the north, where the stray cattle had gone, and an open south end where he could drive his cattle to market or winter range on the flatland. He had chosen the spot when he had been hunting and had found a large herd of elk wintering there. The entire ranch was ringed by mountains, offering protection from the elements and good grazing in summer. The previous year, he had even planted winter wheat and in the spring, potatoes. Pilar used an acre to grow vegetables, which lasted all summer. She and Felicity canned the surplus, which had carried them through the winter.

He had a few hundred acres to the east, in another valley which was protected by high mountains and limestone bluffs. He ran some cattle on it, but they competed with the mule deer and elk, and the game was another resource Brad did not want to lose.

Two days before Brad planned to drive the cattle to the

Arapaho village, Felicity invited Carlos, Pilar, and Julio up to the house for supper. Pilar brought two pies she had baked, and Carlos brought a small bouquet of sunflowers and columbines, which Felicity put into a mason jar filled with water and set in the middle of the large dining table.

After supper, they all sat out on the porch to watch the sunset.

"Do you really think you ought to leave the ranch to drive those cattle to God knows where, Brad?"

Felicity's question surprised him, until he realized that this was why she had prepared such a sumptuous feast for him and his hands. She had wanted to soften him up so she could make her case about the drive north.

"We can use the money," he said. "Until we drive a herd to Denver in the fall, we're pretty cash poor."

"We don't really need money until the end of the year when you can sell some stock."

"Felicity, I made a deal with Walking Crow."

"With an Indian," she said, and Brad's head twisted to look at her.

"Meaning what?" he said.

"Meaning, well, it's not the same, is it?"

"You mean that business between white men is more honorable than business between a white man and an Indian?"

She pulled in a breath. Pilar began to squirm in her chair. Julio slumped in his chair. Carlos looked as if he wanted to sprout wings and fly off the porch.

"I didn't mean it that way exactly," Felicity said.

"I think you did, darlin'. But I forgive you. Old prejudices are hard to shed, I know. But a deal is a deal, and if a man's word isn't any good, then what is?"

"You could wait," she said.

"Wait for what?"

"A better time."

"Did you ever hear someone say 'there's no time like the present'?"

"Oh, my mother, yes. But you know what I mean. Drive those cattle up just before we leave for Denver."

"No, Felicity. I told Wading Crow I'd bring them up right away. Right away is the present. Julio and I leave day after tomorrow."

"I think it's a mistake."

"Why?"

"Those horse tracks. Strange men watching the house at night. Pilar is scared to death. Those men killed her dogs, and she thinks we might be next. After what happened to the Seguins."

"Do you want to live in fear all your life, girl?"

"Don't call me 'girl,'" she snapped. "And, no, I don't want to live in fear. That's why I'm asking you not to go. Not now."

Brad said nothing, but he was fuming, as all could see. He glowered at Felicity, and his eyes narrowed to slits as if to bank the fires within. The sun painted the far clouds in subtle pastels, salmon and pink, gilded some with gold and others with silver. Bats appeared, plying the air with silent leathery wings, their peeping cries guiding them into small clouds of insects. Somewhere a quail piped and the sky began to drain its ocean blue to a pale white-washed gray.

"Pilar, let us go. Thank you for the fine meal, Felicity."

"Good night, Felicity," Pilar said, rising from her chair.

"Don't you want to wait around for the fistfight?" Felicity asked, without sarcasm.

"You two love each other too much for that," Pilar said.

"*Buenas noches,*" Julio said.

"I think I go now, too," Carlos said, and jumped from his chair. "Thank you for the supper. See you tomorrow, Brad."

Brad and Felicity said their good nights, then sat in silence for a while as the sun sank below the snowcapped peaks and the clouds turned to ashen batting. The bats whirred close to the porch and made little squeaking sounds as they devoured mosquitoes.

"Well, I certainly ruined a perfectly good evening," Felicity said after a time.

"No, you didn't." He reached over and covered her hand on the chair's armrest with his. "I see the worth of your concern, Felicity. And I don't want to leave."

"Just think about it, will you, Brad? Think straight through it, and think real hard."

"I'll think about it," he promised.

He told himself he wasn't lying to her. He would think about making that drive. But his mind was made up. He had promised Wading Crow he'd bring him ten head of cattle, and he wanted his word to be good, now and always.

"If you go," she said, "Wading Crow will make you do that Snake Dance. You'll probably get bitten and die. And I'll be a young widow."

"Boo hoo," Brad said. "I'm not going to do no Snake Dance and you're not going to be a widow. You're going to live to be a hundred and so am I."

"Ha," she said, rising from her chair as she slapped at a mosquito that had landed on her neck.

"I'll be in soon," he said.

"Don't be long, Brad."

"That sounds like an invitation."

"It is," she said coyly as she opened the door, and Curly jumped up on her, nearly knocking her down.

Brad watched the night coming on. He would only be gone a week or so. They had been back for a week and nothing had happened. He felt sure that their fears were just so much smoke. Nothing would happen while he was away. Pilar and Felicity could both handle a rifle, and Carlos was a crack shot with a pistol or a rifle. They could drive off any would-be rustlers. And Curly could sound the alarm.

He was sure of it.

He got up to go inside, lingering at the porch railing for a moment.

In the darkness, he did not see the two riders steal along the creek, their horses' hooves wrapped in burlap.

They made no sound. One of them put a pair of binoculars to his eyes and looked at the man on the porch.

The stranger held the binoculars on Brad until he walked inside and closed the door.

Then the man put his binoculars back in the case and turned his horse. The other man followed him as they rode off to the south.

The bats filled their gullets and flew on, down to the beaver dams far below the valley.

And the moon was still asleep somewhere below the high peaks of the Rockies.

FOURTEEN

❧

Ginger was a good cutting horse. Brad let him work, ex-
ulting in the sure-footed way Ginger leaped at the cows,
responding to Brad's every light touch of the reins against
his neck. He never had to use the bit. He could feel Ginger's powerful muscles beneath him as the horse charged,
retreated, swung sideways to cut a cow from the herd. It
was like riding a great and powerful engine that was all
muscle, bone, and sinew. Ginger's performance took Brad's
breath away, and the wind on his face made him feel as if
he were riding at high speed down a mountain slope.

Julio, on his pinto cow pony, Chato, drove the cut-
away steers into the pack where Carlos could manage
them on his horse, Tico. Tico rode a slow circle around
the four head, kept them bunched. Carlos marveled at the
way Ginger focused on each cow, forced it out of the
herd, and sent it toward Julio and Chato. Carlos loved
working with the cattle even though he knew Tico, a part-
Arabian bobtailed dun with a cropped mane, could not
perform the same feats as Ginger. There was the heady

scent of cow dung and animal sweat in the close air of the valley, the tang of chewed grass on the green lips of the cattle. All of it made his blood sing in his veins like some soaring fandango dance in Guanajuato, where he had been born.

Brad cut out a few more head. Ginger drove them to Julio, who passed them off to Carlos. Brad saved the brindle cow for last. She had been eyeing him warily from her own little *querencía*, the spot she had chosen to make her stand and avoid being captured or driven.

"Come on, Ginger," Brad said, and turned the horse in a wide circle to come up behind the brindle. Unless the cow turned its head, it was blind to its rear. Brad reined in Ginger and waited, watching the brindle to see if she would bolt and run or wait him out. He motioned to Julio to move off toward Carlos. Julio turned Chato and rode slowly over to the bunched cattle, nine of them held tight by Tico and Carlos. He pulled up and turned to watch Brad and Ginger. He was sweating under the heat of the spring sun and his shirt clung to his chest as if plastered there.

A meadowlark trilled down by the creek, and mountain quail wallowed in dirt beds, fluttering their wings to dust out the mites. Trout basked in the shallows, watching for flying nymphs or mayflies, and the buzz of flies sawed the silence as they dodged switching cow and horse tails.

Brad watched the brindle. When she stared straight ahead, he ticked Ginger's flanks with his spurs. The horse strode to the brindle's hindside. The cow tried to bolt to the right, but Ginger cut her off, and when she tried to escape to her left, Ginger was on her, towering over her, his legs nimble and quick. He herded the lone cow to the bunch already gathered, and she slid into their midst like a hot knife through butter.

"All right boys," Brad said, "let's run them into the little corral."

The three men herded the ten head of cattle to a small

corral north of the barn. Carlos jumped down and pulled poles to close the gate. Julio held the reins of his horse.

"Let's pack up, Julio, kiss our wives good-bye, and head on out."

Julio nodded and rode off to his bunkhouse.

"You keep an eye on things while I'm gone, Carlos."

"Do not worry, Brad. I will do this."

"I know you will. I'm depending on you."

Carlos patted his pistol and grinned.

"Be back inside of two weeks."

"I will look for you in ten days," Carlos said.

Brad laughed and turned Ginger toward the house. The easy part was over. Now he had to drive ten head of cattle through the mountains, try to make it to the Arapaho village in three days, four at the most.

Felicity was waiting for him when he walked into the house. So was Curly. The dog was all wag, and his body bent like a pretzel as Brad patted him on the head.

"I've got you all packed," she said, entwining his neck with both arms. "Damn you."

"Oh, now you curse me."

"I'm just mighty peeved that you're going on this fool drive."

"You look darn cute when you're peevish," he said, and smacked her on the lips. She clung to him, and her kiss wasn't a smack. It was long and lingering, and he felt more than a tug of desire. He downright wanted her, then and there. She had that effect on him. He squeezed her tight against him, mashing her lips with his, and her breasts set his chest afire.

"You better not look cute to those Indian squaws," she said, pulling away from him to look up into his eyes.

"Don't call them squaws. They're women."

"That's what I'm afraid of," she said.

"Aw, darlin', you don't have to worry about that. I'm as faithful as Curly when it comes to you."

"Curly is faithful to whoever gives him food."

"See?" he said, and she crinkled her nose and cocked her head, gave him a teasing look.

"You be careful, Brad, you hear?"

"I'll be back before you know it. Before you even miss me."

"I miss you already," she said, and broke away to show him what she had packed. The saddlebags lay on the divan. They were bulging. Two wooden canteens lay against them.

"There's food for three days, coffee, a pot, two tin cups, dried beef, cooked pinto beans, bread, some apples, and other stuff you might like."

"Thanks, honey. I appreciate it."

"I wish I were going with you," she said.

"Don't make it any worse than it is, Felicity. It's hard leaving you like this. But I'll bring back gold, and we'll go to town and throw a foofaraw."

"Promise?"

"Cross my heart," he said.

They kissed, and he slung the saddlebags over his shoulder and grabbed the leather straps of the canteens. She walked out the door with him, blocked Curly from leaving, and stood on the porch looking down at him as he put the saddlebags in back of the pommel of his saddle and slung the canteens from his saddle horn, draping one on each side of Ginger. He mounted and raised a hand in farewell, turned his horse toward the corral.

"Keep an eye peeled," he said as he rode off, and wanted to bite his lip. The woman was worried enough, he thought, without him making it worse.

Julio met Brad at the corral. His saddlebags were bulging, too.

"Ready?" Brad said.

"*Listo*," Julio replied.

"Let's take 'em out."

Carlos was there at the pole gate, and Brad motioned for him to pull the gate open to let the cows out. Then he went inside on foot and shooed them all out to the waiting horsemen.

After a few attempts by the cattle to break ranks and return to the main herd, the two men got the cows moving up to the timber and out of sight of the herd.

Brad knew where to find the first canyon and the trail that Wading Crow had drawn for him. The canyon curved from east to west, then opened to the trail to the north. He had the map vividly in his mind. He would go over it again and again on the drive, seeing Wading Crow with his stick, marking the trails and the landmarks.

They made a good ten miles that day through rugged country. Brad enjoyed the open sky and the mountains, the clean fresh air, the scent of pines, and an occasional jet of bear scat that spooked the horses and the cattle. He thought he saw a cougar on the rimrock but could not tell if it was shadow or substance. It was great country, and he loved every mile of it.

The cattle were trailwise at the end of the first day, and they stopped by a marked spring before sunset. The spring was right where Wading Crow had said it would be, and there was a small niche in the limestone bluff where the cattle could bed down. They stretched rope between two scrub pines that flanked the depression and laid out their bedrolls right in front of the ropes.

Julio built a fire. There were already stones in a circle and burned ground, plenty of squaw wood and downed limbs nearby.

"It's a fine camp, Julio," Brad said as they were munching on hardtack, dried beef, and wizened apples.

"Will the others be this good?"

"Shouldn't have but one or two more."

"We are heading north?"

"North and a little westerly, maybe."

"You do not know?"

"I know enough to get us there."

There was a silence between them for a time. But Brad

could see that Julio had something on his mind. The Mexican brought out a plug of tobacco and cut off a piece. He offered the plug and his knife to Brad.

"Don't mind if I do," Brad said. He cut off a chew and stuck it in a corner of his mouth. "That coffee boiled yet?"

"It takes long to boil," Julio said. "It is high here."

"It's high everywhere up here in the Rockies."

"Yes," Julio agreed.

"Good chaw," Brad said, and sent a flume of tobacco juice flying toward a rock.

"Do you not have worry about leaving the women and Carlos to watch the ranch?" Julio asked.

"Worry never gets you nowhere."

"But I have worry."

"Does it help to worry, Julio?"

"It helps the guilt, I think."

Brad smiled.

"It grows gray hair, too."

"Or pulls it out, maybe."

They both laughed.

"Look, Julio, let's not talk about what we left back there anymore. The trip is long enough without keeping our minds in two places at once. Let's just tend to our business, enjoy the ride, and we can break out the whiskey when we get back home. Okay?"

"Okay, if you say so, Brad. Still, I have the worry."

"Big or small?"

Julio grinned.

"It is a small worry," he admitted.

"Good. Keep it small. Maybe it will go away."

Later, Brad said he would take the first watch. Julio went to sleep, and Brad sat there alone, his rifle close at hand. He heard the chorus of wolves far in the distance and marveled at how big the moon was when it rose. He'd had a beautiful sunset to cap the day, and the coffee hadn't been too bitter.

He tried not to think of Felicity, but that was impossible.

He thought of her. He thought of her until he woke Julio and long before he finally went to sleep.

He missed her, her loving touch, her soft hair, and her dazzling smile. After only one day, he thought.

And he, too, had a small worry.

FIFTEEN

∾

Early the next morning, shortly after breaking camp, Brad picked up the tracks of the Arapaho. The trail was marred with travois furrows, unshod hoof marks, blurred but discernible since there had been no rain for more than a week.

"We must be on the right trail," Julio said.

"You doubted me?"

"You said you had no map."

"Oh, I have a map, Julio." He touched a finger to his forehead. "It's right up here."

"I hope your memory is long enough to take us back home."

"It's supposed to last that long. We'll see."

The cattle moved well, with little prodding, and the brindle cow did not try to run off. They left the trail at times to let the cattle graze as they walked, but always kept the trail in sight and close. The cows were a mix of Herefords and other breeds; one or two had longhorn ancestors far back in the family tree. These were shorthorns, of sturdy stock, and Brad knew they would not lose much weight on the short drive.

They made about fifteen miles the second day, which surprised Brad because they were following a circuitous route. From the looks of the trail, he knew it must have been used for centuries by migrating herds of buffalo, mountain men, and native hunters. A surveyor could not have found a better place to build a road through the mountains, and he wondered if it might not have been carved by an ancient river and, for some reason, left to turn dry and barren. He could picture a river running its course down through the mountains, but as he had learned, rivers changed courses, dried up, or went underground.

They crossed small creeks and grassy meadows, surprisingly lush, and Brad lost the travois tracks for a time when they passed through a small moraine strewn with boulders, more evidence that a vigorous river had once flowed through that part of the country. There were mule deer feeding in one of the glens and plenty of animal sign along the way, and once, when he looked at a towering mountain just above the timberline, he saw a Rocky Mountain sheep, a ram with a massive set of horns curled like a war helmet around his head. But always, he found the travvy tracks and knew he was on the right path.

They spent the second night in a grassy sward where the Arapahos had camped. The cattle grazed most of the night, drank at a small spring, and none strayed. That was the thing about a herd, Brad thought, it clung together in fair weather or foul, and as long as it was peaceable, they were content to travel or graze. He was very pleased that such a small bunch would get along so well.

On the third day, Brad and Julio started out early, just before dawn. It was light enough to see the tracks of those who had gone before, but by noon, the tracks faded out. Completely.

"Where do we go now?" Julio asked.

"I still have Wading Crow's map in my head," he said.

"But there are no more tracks."

"Yeah, Julio. It's as if they all vanished into thin air. But we know better, don't we?"

They were surrounded by low hills and high mountains just beyond. There was a semblance of a trail there, but it petered out a few yards from where the tracks just disappeared.

Brad rode a wide circle while Julio held the herd, and some distance away from the trail, he saw a fairly fresh stump of a limb high up on a spruce tree. Hard to see. He rode around some more and spotted other slashes where a long branch had been cut from a juniper and another spruce.

He sat there, pondering what it all meant, then finally returned to where Julio was waiting with the ten head of cattle.

"You see that spruce over yonder, Julio?" Brad pointed to a nearby tree, a fully limbed and handsome spruce tree.

"I see it," Julio said.

"If you were to cut off one of those long branches, what would you have?"

"I do not know, Brad. Just a branch, I think."

"Or maybe a broom."

"You mean a broom to sweep the floor with?"

"Or to sweep away tracks in sand and dirt."

Brad pretended he was sweeping with a broom.

Julio's face lit up and his eyes widened in their sockets until they looked like oversized marbles.

"That is why the tracks go?"

"I think so. They cut branches and swept away all traces of the travvy and their horses. The ground is as smooth as a hen's egg, bald as a billiard ball."

Julio stared at the ground all around him.

"You do not even see the sweeps."

"No, they did a good job in erasing everything, just somehow left no needle marks on the ground."

"*Indios*," Julio said, and crossed himself. "*Diablos, por seguro.*"

"No, just *muy sabio*. Very smart. They don't want anyone to follow their tracks to their village."

"Secrets," Julio said.

"Well, let's honor their need for secrecy and cut us some spruce bows, tie them to our saddle horns, and sweep away our tracks."

"That is much work and will delay us."

"You know what the boy rabbit said to the girl rabbit, Julio?"

"No."

"He said, 'This won't take long, did it?' And, so, let's get to it."

The two men took turns cutting spruce and juniper boughs in another place. Julio cursed as he tried to climb an unclimbable tree, crying out each time a bough struck him in the eye or slapped him on the face. His hands were sticky from sap, and he got the sap on his trousers and his face, his shirt and on his saddle horn. Brad did not fare much better. He thought the Arapahos must have had small, thin boys along to do the cutting, or small trained monkeys.

But they cut six boughs and lashed them together and rode crisscross behind the cattle to remove their tracks. When Brad looked back he could see the marks the limbs made, but he knew the wind would take care of those in time.

Late in the afternoon, they entered a big valley ringed by mountains on one side and tall bluffs on the other. There were game trails through it and a lively creek running its entire length. The cattle wanted to stop and graze, but Brad looked up beyond a grassy promontory and saw a huge granite mountain. At least it looked monolithic. A butte, he thought. Just like Wading Crow had described it.

They drove the cattle up the valley, then up to a wide shelf, then turned toward the massive butte. They rode through timber and avoided the deadfalls. Some of the rocks resembled ancient ruins, moss-covered as they were and clustered with climbing plants that might have been wild vines. He could not tell. But it was an eerie place to be with night coming on and only thin game trails crossing their path. The butte loomed even larger the closer they

got to it. Below them, the valley looked serene and unin-
habited by game or folk, and then, beyond the trees, a wide,
flat plain, rocky and forbidding, stretched all the way to
the butte and beyond. There were other limestone bluffs to
the right of the lone butte.

As they emerged from the trees, there was a rustling
sound, followed by a number of other sounds.

A man appeared before them, on foot, his right hand
raised high. He carried a bow with an arrow nocked to
his string. He was naked except for a beaded loincloth and
beaded moccasins.

"Hold up, Julio," Brad said, and rode to the flank of the
cows.

"You, white man," the Arapaho brave said, "where you
go?"

"I bring these cattle to Wading Crow."

Then Brad and Julio saw a number of other warriors,
all armed with short bows and wearing quivers on their
backs. They all had their arrows nocked to their bow-
strings.

The two realized that they were completely surrounded.

"I think they will shoot, Brad," Julio said.

"Just stay calm. Wading Crow must have told them we
were coming."

"One is aiming at me."

"Don't go for your rifle or draw your pistol, Julio. Just
wait."

"I am doing the piss in my pants," Julio said.

"I'm about to piss mine, too," Brad said.

The leader came closer. He looked belligerent, and
Brad was reminded of animals that swelled their bodies
to look larger when threatened, like the porcupine or the
prairie chicken.

"White man," the man yelled. "What name?"

"My name?"

"You name."

"Brad . . ." He started to say. Then he made the Indian
sign for the snake. "Sidewinder," he said.

"You come. Bring cow."

The man turned and Brad nodded to Julio.

"We'll follow him," he said.

The other braves fell in on both sides of them, as if they were escorts, and they followed the leader out onto the rocky plain and along a path that led to a saddleback behind the butte. They climbed onto the saddleback and then onto the butte itself.

Brad looked down and was surprised at the commanding view he had of the valley and the far bluffs. Anyone atop that butte could see enemies coming for miles.

Then they saw it, in the center of the butte, teepees in a circle, women and children gathered outside the ring, men standing stolid and still watching the small clutch of cattle and the two white men riding behind them, with armed braves on both flanks. None made a sound.

"I do not see Wading Crow," Julio said, a terrified quaver in his voice. "Maybe this is not his village."

"If it's not, Julio, we're in a heap of trouble. Your hair on tight?"

"Do not joke me, Brad. I am now scared pissless."

"That's a good way to be, I think. Better than pissing your pants."

"I do not like this."

"Do you know any Arapaho words?" Brad asked.

"You know I do not."

"Me, neither, but what little sign I know doesn't include Wading Crow's. I might hop around like a bird and lift my feet like I'm wading a creek. But if that doesn't work . . ."

"Then what?" Julio asked.

"Ever see a man grow gray hair inside of ten seconds? That will be me."

"You do not calm my fears, Brad."

"Well, nobody's shot us yet."

The leader stopped and turned around. He held up his hand again.

"What now?" Brad asked.

The man didn't answer. Then Brad heard a horse whicker and what sounded like the moo of a cow, the bleat of a sheep. Beyond the teepees, he saw movement. Small boys rode toward them on Indian ponies, and they all carried ropes. He saw something that looked like a corral made of stacked, crisscrossed timber with small animals inside.

The boys on horseback rode up to the herd and stopped. They began to make loops in their ropes.

"They are going to take the cows," Julio said.

"Well, they can have them. I wonder where in hell Wading Crow is."

"He is not here."

The leader strode back to Brad's horse and grabbed the side strap of his bridle. He gestured for Brad to dismount. At the same time, one of the braves caught hold of Julio's bridle and pulled on his boot. "Down, down," he said in English. Julio dismounted a moment after Brad's boots touched the ground.

"Me called Green Turtle," the leader said to Brad. "Wading Crow brother."

"Did you hear that, Julio? This is Wading Crow's brother."

The men around Julio began to laugh and pointed to his crotch. They made obscene gestures and flapped their loincloths, exposing themselves.

Julio hung his head in shame and did not answer.

For him, the world had turned hostile. He was surrounded by armed savages who carried bows and arrows, and big knives on their beaded belts. They were making fun of him.

He just wanted to sink into the ground and disappear.

Green Turtle started to lead Ginger away, toward the village.

"Sidewinder follow," he said.

As they left, the boys threw their loops and had all the cattle captured, each one separately.

Brad wanted to ask where Wading Crow was, but before he could speak, one of the braves who had escorted them up to the top of the butte ran up to him and struck Brad with his bow.

Then he let out a bloodcurdling yell, and the others charged up to him and pummeled his back and legs with their bows, all screeching in high-pitched voices.

Brad went to his knees.

And before he knew it, his right hand was streaking for the butt of his pistol.

His eyes narrowed to slits, and his jaw turned granite. Rage enveloped him.

He was ready to kill.

SIXTEEN

❧

Brad pulled his Colt free of its holster, cocking the hammer back with his thumb so quick all the Indians saw was a blur. He leveled the barrel at the head of the nearest man, the last Arapaho to strike him with his bow. Then he stood up and pulled the set of rattles up, shook them in the hapless Arapaho's face. The braves all drew back as if struck by an invisible current of electricity. The whirring sound of the rattles filled them all with fear.

Then, to Julio's and Brad's surprise, all of the braves began to shout and jump up and down, smiles on their faces.

Brad held his finger curled just short of the trigger. He drew a shallow breath, beads of sweat breaking out on his forehead.

Then the Arapahos all turned toward the village.

Walking toward Brad was a lone figure. Wading Crow strode up, the crowd parting to let him through. He looked at Brad, and Brad held his gaze.

Brad shook the rattles again.

Indians nearby sucked in their breaths.

Then, silence, as the rattles stood still.

"Welcome, Sidewinder, to my village," Wading Crow said. "You have much big medicine with my people."

Brad lowered his pistol and eased the hammer to half cock.

"A hell of a welcome, Wading Crow."

"They fear you, my people, and they honor you by striking you with their bows. They want some of your medicine."

"They can have all they want without beating me to a pulp."

"Come, let us sit and smoke."

Brad looked over at Julio. He was frozen in place, his face a lurid, bloodless mask, his lips clamped together.

"Come on, Julio. We're going to parley with Wading Crow."

Julio uttered an expletive in Spanish. Some of the color returned to his cheeks.

Brad slid his pistol back in its holster.

"You draw the pistol quick," Wading Crow said. "And you have shoot in your eyes."

"I didn't want to shoot that man."

"But, you were ready."

"I was ready," Brad said, and wondered if he really would have pulled the trigger. If any of the braves had moved or threatened him, he knew he would have dropped at least one or two of them. When a man was faced with danger, he defended himself or he lost the fight. Sometimes a bluff was as good as a straight flush.

As the Arapaho led their horses away and the boys pulled the cattle toward the corral in back of the village, Brad walked with Wading Crow and some of the other braves into the village. There, he saw women and children, all standing as silent as statues. Some of the women bowed to him, and he nodded his head in return. The children, open-mouthed, just stared at him in awe.

Brad was surprised to see the women striking the teepees at the other end of the village. They were stripping the poles of hides and stacking the poles. Others folded the deer and elk hides. They were systematic and efficient.

"You are breaking camp," Brad said to Wading Crow.

"By the time the sun goes to sleep, the village will be gone."

"Where are you going?"

"To a secret place. We stay here only three days until you come. Then we go."

"No Snake Dance?"

"Snake Dance secret, too. Much fasting. Much ceremony."

Brad was relieved.

Wading Crow ushered them into the nearest teepee. Inside, he saw Gray Owl sitting cross-legged on a woven blanket. Before him he had three bowls and a large sack. He was pouring what was in the sack into the three clay bowls.

"Do not speak with Gray Owl," Wading Crow said.

"What's he doing?" Brad asked as he sat down. Julio sat next to him, his gazed fixed on Gray Owl, who was nearly naked and wore a brightly colored headband.

"He bless the cornmeal. Make it holy for Snake Dance."

"Must be quite a ceremony."

Wading Crow looked puzzled. He did not know what the word "ceremony" meant, Brad thought.

"Much to do," Brad explained.

"Gray Owl, Snake Priest. Much big medicine."

Wading Crow took a long pipe from what looked like a small quiver but was really only a beaded leather case to hold the pipe. He offered tobacco to the four directions, filled the pipe, and lit it. He smoked, spewed bluish plumes of smoke to the four directions, then handed the pipe to Brad. Brad puffed it, blew out the smoke, then handed it to Julio, who did the same thing before handing the pipe back to Wading Crow.

Two of the braves came in carrying Julio's and Brad's rifles. They presented them to the two white men, then backed out of the teepee. Brad could hear the lodge poles falling, being stacked, and the rustle of hides as they were stripped and folded.

"I thank you for the cattle," Wading Crow said. "Much meat for people."

"I must return to my home," Brad said.

Wading Crow set the pipe down on the firering stones and reached in back of him. He brought forth a set of brass scales and set them on the ground in front of him.

"Dust or nuggets?" Wading Crow asked.

"Dust."

"Blow away in wind."

"No, I'll keep it safe."

Wading Crow beamed. He reached behind the sash around his waist and pulled out a heavy pouch.

"Have pouch?"

Brad shook his head.

Wading Crow reached behind him again and brought out a small leather pouch with a leather drawstring. He handed it to Brad.

"You keep," Wading Crow said.

Brad took the sack, set it down. He and Julio watched as Wading Crow started eking out gold dust from the sack in his hand. He put a counterweight on one of the scales.

"Four ounces," Wading Crow said.

When the scales balanced from the first pouring, Wading Crow held out a hand for Brad's empty sack. He lifted the small cup of gold dust and poured it into the empty sack. He performed this same procedure until he had measured out twenty ounces of gold dust. Then he pulled the drawstring tight and handed the bulging sack to Brad.

"Thank you, Wading Crow," he said.

"Good," Wading Crow said. "You eat?"

Brad shook his head. He could hear the teepee next to Wading Crow's going down. The rustle of sewn hides, the crash of poles to the earth, the footpads of the women and children.

Gray Owl finished blessing the meal, dusted his hands together, then poured the meal back into the sack.

"Sidewinder," he said. "It is good my eyes have seen you this day."

"It's good to see you, Gray Owl. You caught enough snakes?"

"Thirty snake," Gray Owl said. "They sleep. Soon, they dance."

Brad was glad he wasn't going to be around for that particular ritual.

He used his hands to sign as he spoke to Wading Crow.

"Soon, the sun will set, Wading Crow. Julio and I will go. We must ride fast to our home and our women."

"Yes," Gray Owl said, which surprised Brad, since he had spoken to Wading Crow.

He turned to look at the Hopi.

There was an odd expression on Gray Owl's face and smoky light in his eyes. He looked up through the smoke hole of the teepee and closed his eyes for a moment, then leveled his gaze at Brad.

"You go quick," he said.

Brad looked at Wading Crow.

"Is Gray Owl telling Sidewinder something?" he said.

"Gray Owl wise man. Snake Priest. Him know many things. Him see far. Him see over mountains."

"Does he see my home?"

Gray Owl's eyes rolled back in their sockets. He seemed to go into a kind of trance as he closed his eyes, and rocked back and forth in silence.

"What is it, Gray Owl?" Brad asked. "What do you see?"

Gray Owl said nothing. He just kept rocking back and forth.

Brad felt a tug on his arm. He turned to look at Julio.

"*Vamanos*," Julio whispered. "Let us go."

"I want to hear what Gray Owl has to say," Brad said.

"You wait," Wading Crow said. "Gray Owl see far. Gray Owl looking."

It was agony for Brad to wait while the Hopi rocked back and forth, his eyes closed. Brad felt as if he were a prisoner waiting to hear his sentence from an incompetent judge. He wiped sweat from around his neck, and had the urge to grab the Hopi and shake him until he spoke.

Finally, Gray Owl opened his eyes.

"Sidewinder," he said. "Give me your rattles."

Brad looked down, but the rattles were inside his shirt. He pulled them out, took the sinew from around his neck, and handed the rattles to Gray Owl.

Gray Owl took them, then reached into the sack. His fist came back with meal, and he held the rattles in one hand, sprinkled the holy meal on the rattles, then returned the remaining meal to the sack. He said something in the Hopi language, closed his eyes, then opened them. He handed the rattles back to Brad.

"Keep safe, Sidewinder. Much medicine now. You go home."

"What did you see, Gray Owl?" Brad asked as he draped the sinew with the rattles around his neck.

"Many cattle running. Many men riding horse. Hair of woman flying in the wind. Me see empty house. Me see dog spirit rising. That is all."

"What does he say?" Julio asked.

"I don't know," Brad said. "I don't take much stock in it. Injun stuff maybe."

"I do not like his words," Julio muttered.

Brad tucked the pouch of gold inside his belt and stood up with his rifle.

"Good luck, Wading Crow," Brad said in Spanish. "Come see me if you want more cattle before the snow flies."

"I will come," Wading Crow said.

Brad said good-bye to Gray Owl, whose eyes were wet and rheumy as if he had rubbed cornmeal into them. He had a sad look on his face as he held his hand up in fare-well.

The horses were waiting outside, held by two young braves. There was only one teepee still standing, the one they had been in. When Gray Owl and Wading Crow stepped outside, some women and young girls went inside and came out carrying blankets, robes, rugs, and other goods. They bundled them up in a large buffalo robe. None of them spoke, and Brad clucked to Ginger and ticked his flanks with his spurs. He and Julio rode back toward the saddleback.

When Brad looked back, the teepee was gone. He saw Arapaho braves tying their travois to horses and others riding toward the corrals.

The noises of the fading village died away as the two men rode down into the valley. The sky was streaked with gray and golden clouds; the sun was about three fingers from the jagged mountain horizon. A mule deer jumped away from the creek as the two men passed by, and dark birds flew along its length, heading east.

"I have worry," Julio said, as they rode through the timber at the far end of the valley.

"About what?"

"About what that Hopi said."

"What do you think he said?" Brad asked.

"I do not know."

"Neither do I," Brad said, but he knew how Julio felt. There was something ominous in the Hopi's words, something deeply disturbing. It was as if Gray Owl was looking into the future and seeing something ominous. The empty house, a woman's hair flying in the wind, a dead dog. Past, present, or future?

For now, Brad couldn't get home fast enough.

SEVENTEEN

~

The men had started grumbling the night before. Now, an hour before daylight, Delbert Coombs was kicking them out of their bedrolls in their dry camp. His brother, Hiram, was the first to get up, the first to curse the darkness and the cold.

"Damn it, Del, you don't wake a man without'n you have a cup of hot coffee in your hand."

"If I did, Hiram, I'd pour it all over your sorry pate. Now, get up and start saddlin' horses."

Two other men got up, their mouths sticky with dried tobacco juice, their throats sore from breathing through their mouths all night.

"What now, Delbert?" Abner Wicks asked. "We done checked that ranch for two days runnin'. I tell you they ain't nobody there 'ceptin' for two wimmin, a Mex, and one old curly-haired dog."

"That's right," Ridley Smoot said. "Them cattle is strung out all over creation just waitin' to be gathered."

"I want you two to check one more time, Abner, before sunrise, and then, if the time is right, we'll jump 'em all."

The other two men, Fred Raskin and Tod "Toad" Sutphen, crawled out of their bedrolls last. Toad scratched his beard stubble, and the sound was so loud it sounded like sandpaper rubbing over a chunk of cross-grained hickory. Raskin got up and walked a few yards into the draw and urinated on the limestone wall.

"You sound like a cow pissin' on a flat rock, Freddie," Sutphen said.

"Drank too much branch water last night," Raskin said, buttoning up his dirty trousers.

"You'll shed those coats when that sun comes up," Hiram said to the men. He came back leading two horses. "Here you go, Ridley." He handed the bitter end of the reins to Smoot. "Abner, take your'n and mount up. Time's a-wastin'."

"Hiram," Wicks said, "if'n my fist wasn't froze up, I'd wring your damned neck."

"Yeah, and if I had a quirt handy, I'd stripe your backside with forty lashes."

"Quit the bitchin'," Delbert Coombs said. "Let's get to gettin'. We'll be waitin' down at the far end of the crick when you boys get through scoutin'. Now, I don't want them women touched. Shoot the Mex. Make sure he's stone dead, then help us."

"You aim to kidnap them wimmin?" Hiram said to his brother.

"We'll have some fun with them and keep 'em hostage in case Storm tracks us."

"Mighty risky," Hiram said.

"What ain't?" Delbert said as the two men rode off toward the Storm ranch. The others saddled their horses and rubbed out all traces of the dry camp, which weren't much, and gave their horses handfuls of grain.

"Don't give 'em too much," Hiram said. "We don't want no founderin' when we run them cattle."

"Just enough to flatten their bellies," Delbert added. "Check your pistols and rifles. And follow me."

Wicks and Smoot rode to the creek in full darkness. They rode slow and careful. They knew the way, having scouted the ranch for nearly a month, mostly in the early morning and at night. They rode right to the spot where they had the best view of the main house and both bunk-houses. They reined up in a copse of aspen and alder bushes. Smoot took the binoculars out of his saddlebags and strung them over his neck with gloved hands. There was a chill in the air but no breeze.

There were no lamps lit in any of the dwellings. The first light to show was in the little bunkhouse where the Mexican stayed. They knew his name was Carlos something. Delbert had told them. He knew all of their names. He'd had his eye on this ranch and these cattle for a long time.

"The Mex is gettin' up," Smoot said.

"Yeah, he'll boil him some coffee, and then go to the stables and saddle up."

"Or go see that Mex gal, Pilar. She might even cook him some breakfast." He laughed a leering laugh.

"She can pull my rope any time she wants," Wicks said.

"You ain't got no rope to pull, Abner," Ridley said.

"We better be quiet. We don't want to give the Mex no warnin'."

They were quiet as they waited for the sun to rise, the creek layered with a foggy, cool blanket, wisps of mist rising off the waters. A trout broke the surface and both men jumped at the slap of water. They drew into their coats and slumped in their saddles to keep their warmth from escaping. In the glint of moonlight, they could see their breaths, soft steam clouds that evaporated inches from their faces.

A light breeze floated down from the high range, waft-ing perfume to the watchers as the flowers released their aromas. The two men shrugged deeper into their wool-lined coats, pulled their collars up, and stuck their gloved hands back in their coat pockets. The horses nibbled water at the edge of the creek, a coyote yipped to the south of them, and an answering chorus of high-pitched yodels sounded from somewhere deep in the timber.

A lamp suddenly came lit in the other bunkhouse. A few minutes later, they saw yellow light through a window in the big house, and smoke streamed from the chimney.

"They're rousin' up," Wick said.

"Seems like."

"You watch the Mex's bunkhouse. I'll keep an eye on the main house."

"You got the binocs."

"Want 'em?"

"Naw, you keep 'em. I got eyes like a buzzard."

"I got eyes like a hawk."

"Buzzards see better."

"They don't see. They smell."

The talk between Ridley and Abner died down as the eastern horizon began to lighten almost imperceptibly. The men wriggled their toes inside their boots to warm them, and the horses took to the grass, pulling up clumps of green, wallowing them in their mouths before cutting them with their teeth. Their bits clacked as they worried the grass before swallowing the masticated mash.

Carlos emerged from his bunkhouse. He stood outside for a moment. He looked over at Julio's bunkhouse, then turned and walked toward the barn, much to Ridley's surprise.

"He ain't goin' over to the other bunkhouse," he said. "Headin' for the barn, looks like."

"Keep your shirt on," Abner said. "He's probably goin' up there to pee."

"I hope he don't saddle up and start snoopin' around them cattle."

"We seen enough. Let's go find Delbert."

"Sure enough," Ridley said. "Be full light right soon."

The two men rode down to the other end of the creek at the south end of the pasture.

"They're all up," Abner said to Delbert. "The Mex went

back to the barn, the two wimmin are inside cookin' break-fast."

"Let's ride up on the south side of the main house. Me and Hiram will get the Storm gal. Ridley, you track down that Mex. The rest of you grab the Mex woman. We'll tie 'em both up and saddle up their horses."

"And then?" Abner asked.

"And then we gather up that herd and hightail it to the corrals."

"With the wimmin?" Ridley asked.

"Yeah, in case Storm and that other Mex comes back a-lookin'."

They broke into three groups and rode toward the ranch headquarters. The sky paled to a soft gray, and the stars began to die out like frozen fireflies. The eastern horizon turned scarlet and yellow along a cream fissure in the sky. Objects took on definition. Bushes and cattle appeared out of the darkness, trees took on shapes, and the grass was tinged with an uncertain light, as if the footlights of a stage were slowly turned higher.

Ridley eased his horse around the main house and headed for the barn. He pulled his rifle from its scabbard as he rounded the house. Hiram and Delbert dismounted at the side of the house and walked to the back door, their boots crunching on light gravel.

The other riders made their way to Julio's bunkhouse, their backs lit by the slowly rising sun, the rumps of their horses glistening like dark palettes smeared with daubs of multicolored paint.

The back door was unlocked. Delbert opened it, put his finger to his lips as he turned to his brother.

He entered the house. A lamp burned in the kitchen, and the wood stove crackled with fresh kindling in the firebox. His footsteps made the boards creak as he walked toward the hall.

Felicity came out of the bedroom, saw the silhouetted shape of Delbert Coombs.

"Brad? How come you came in the back door?"

Delbert drew his pistol. Cocked it.

"Guess again, Missus Storm," he said.

Felicity froze.

Curly, who had been curled up in front of the fireplace in the living room, came up behind her, tail wagging. The dog brushed against her legs as he walked toward Delbert.

Delbert didn't hesitate. Just as Curly was about to leap up on him in a friendly manner, he aimed his pistol and shot him in the head. Curly made no sound as blood spurted from his eye and forehead. He fell to the floor, blood streaming from his head. His hind legs twitched. He gave a short gasp and went limp.

Felicity screamed as Delbert stepped toward her.

She turned to run, and he grabbed one of her arms. He jerked her off her feet and dragged her down the hall. She kicked and screamed.

"You make it hard," Delbert said, "and I'll make it hard. How'd you like a gun barrel bashin' in your face, lady?"

"You bastard. Let go of me," she shouted.

"Better give what I said some thought, Missy. I can shut that mouth of yours with one swipe of my Colt."

"Bastard," she hissed, and he jerked her to her feet.

"You got some of that tie rope, Hiram?" Delbert asked.

"In my pocket."

"Get it out and tie her hands behind her back."

Felicity looked at the two men.

She had never seen either of them before.

"Where's Brad?" she asked. "What have you done with him?"

She realized a second later that it was the wrong thing to say. Brad was up in the mountains, probably riding back from the Arapaho village. Probably close by.

"So, you don't know where your man is, eh?" Delbert said. "That makes it easy."

"He—he's here. I mean he's coming. He's—he's . . ."

"Oh, shut up," Delbert said.

Hiram tied her hands behind her back with store twine. Tightened the double knot.

"That'll fix her, Del," he said.

"To the barn," Delbert said, and walked out the back door. Hiram and Felicity were behind him. Hiram pushed the barrel of his pistol into the center of her back.

"Just so's you know, I don't mind blowin' a hole in a woman," he said in his gruff voice. "In fact, I'd like to do just that if you act up any."

"I'm sure you would," Felicity said, her throat constricted with fear, her anger like a furnace in her mind.

They met the others with Pilar in tow, her hands tied behind her back. She was spitting and cursing in rapid Spanish until one of the men clouted her with his fist.

"Pilar, I'm so sorry," Felicity said as the two groups came together.

"Julio will kill you," Pilar screamed. "He will kill you all."

"Be quiet," Delbert said, "or you'll be beggin' for your life."

"*Cabrón*," Pilar said. "Bastard."

They all stopped outside the barn.

"Ridley?" Delbert called.

There was no answer.

He called Ridley again, louder.

From behind the barn they all heard him answer.

"Comin', Del," he said.

A few minutes later, he walked through the barn, out of breath and panting.

"You kill the Mex?" Delbert asked.

"He—he got clean away. Hell, I chased after him, but he was quick as a damned fox."

"You dumb cluck," Delbert said. "Was he packin'?"

"I don't know. He must've heard me, 'cause he ran like a deer out the back of the barn. Up in the timber. Hell, it'd take a week to find him."

"Saddle up two horses," Delbert ordered. "You men put these gals up on 'em and keep 'em in sight. They try to get away, shoot 'em."

"Yeah, boss," Smoot said. He and Ridley went in the barn.

"Let's get after them cattle," Delbert said. "Time's a-wastin'."

Felicity's jaw tightened as she realized what was happening. She and Brad were about to lose their herd. These men were killers, and no telling what they planned to do with her and Pilar.

And, where was Brad?

What would he find when he came back?

Nothing, she thought, nothing at all except a dead dog and an empty pasture.

She started to cry and hated herself for showing such a weakness. She wanted to cry out, but she knew it would do no good.

These were hard men, and would not hesitate to kill her and Pilar.

Had Carlos gotten away? She hoped so. For she knew in her heart that they wouldn't take him prisoner.

That man who had shot Curly, he would kill Carlos without batting an eye.

She shivered at the thought, and the sadness over Curly welled up in her like a fountain of grief.

And the tears kept coming as something inside her began to die.

EIGHTEEN

❦

Delbert Coombs licked his pudgy lips when he rode to the north end of the pasture, counting heads of cattle. Behind him trailed his brother, Hiram, his belly sagging over his belt like a ball of blubber, an unlit cheroot in his mouth. Coming up in the rear was Ridley Smoot, a bone-thin, wiry man with a protruding Adam's apple that appeared to all but puncture his throat. He was small but deadly, and wore two Smith & Wesson six-guns on his belt, each a .38 caliber. He was kidded by the others for packing such small pistols, but he said that anything heavier would snap his bony wrists and cripple him for life.

Delbert reined up his horse before he reached the north end of the valley. He turned to face the others who halted their horses.

"Toad," he said to Tod Sutphen, "all I want you to do is ride along the timber with your Sharps at the ready. If you see that Mex, shoot him between the eyes."

Sutphen was the best rifle shot in the group. His three days of beard covered most of the scars on his face, the pocks a result of a childhood skin disease. His bulbous nose was pocked as well, with ugly bumps that he continually popped and squeezed to push out the pus. He grew boils on the back of his thick neck that had to be lanced periodically. But his deep-sunk eyes were like an eagle's, and he could shoot a blowfly off a fence post at ten yards.

"I'd dearly love to get me a Mex," Sutphen said. "Make a terbacky pouch out of his nuts."

He cut away from the others and rode his mottled gray horse up behind the barn and began patrolling all along the line of timber, looking for any scant movement, listening for any human sound coming from the trees. The butt of his Sharps rested on his leg, the safety off.

"The rest of you fan out and bunch the cows toward the center of the valley," Delbert said. "We don't want them stampeding across the creek. Ridley, you and Fred take the right flank. Work 'em slow."

"Got it, boss," Ridley said, tweaking his brushy mustache with two fingers. He had lifeless pale blue eyes that always seemed as vacant as smoky glass marbles, and his chin came to a sharp point below a thatch of beard that he kept trimmed with a straight razor. His bloodless lips held a dangling, hand-rolled quirley. "Let's go, Freddie."

Fred Raskin, a wizened, bow-legged man in his forties, with thinning hair—looked fifty, with his pinched face, deep lines across his forehead and on his stubbled chin—followed Smoot as he broke away from the others.

"I'll take the women with me," Delbert said, "teach 'em how to drive cattle."

"One thing, nice, Del," Raskin said.

"Well, look at them cattle. We can sell their hides. They ain't got no brand on 'em. Just ear markings."

"Yeah, we can cut off their ears and nobody'll know where they came from."

"More money," Raskin said.

"You bet," and Delbert's eyes danced with light. The light of pure greed.

The riders fanned out along the far reaches of the long

valley and began the drive, working very slowly. Those along the creek ran the cattle toward the center of the pasture, and those nearest the timber and the houses pushed those cattle down to mingle with the others. As the herd grew in size, it began to amble south in the direction Delbert wanted them to go.

Felicity looked at the terrified Pilar. Pilar's face was still wet with tears, and she seemed on the verge of collapse. Delbert had to prod her horse with a kick to make her move. Although her hands were tied, she was squeezing her knees into the horse to make it turn and balk. Both women had their feet tied to the stirrups, so they couldn't jump down and make a run for it.

Pilar will fight to her death, Felicity thought, but didn't voice it.

Her own mind was processing possibilities at a high speed. She was glad that Carlos had gotten away. Perhaps he would track them later, and then go back and tell Brad where they had been taken. She wondered if Carlos had a pistol or rifle with him. Maybe he would kill the man they called Toad, and there would be one less for Brad and Julio to deal with when the time came.

She thought about Curly and how he had died. He had just wanted to be friendly with that Delbert, and the man had shot him dead. Poor Curly never had a chance.

And what would Brad think when he got back and saw that all the cattle were gone and Curly was dead? Unless Carlos survived and told him some of what happened, he would never know.

And she might never see Brad again.

She had no idea who these men were or where they were from, but she thought they might be the same ones who murdered the Seguin family, stole all their cattle, and burned their home down. The thought gave her a shudder. She might eventually suffer the same fate as poor Mrs. Seguin, her husband, and her children.

She also wondered what Pilar was thinking. She just hoped she wouldn't do something rash. These men were killers and wouldn't hesitate to shoot her if she got out of line.

The morning sun rose in the sky and the coolness left the ground. A meadowlark trilled at the far end of the valley, and birds flew overhead. She could hear the jays squabbling up in the woods, and beneath it all, the mumbling tumble of the creek as it rolled past exposed stones, a faint gurgling that spoke of life and the orderly system of the universe itself.

The men said little. They were good at herding and driving. They were obviously experienced with cattle, even though Felicity knew them to be outlaws. Common thieves. She hated every one of them, and her anger was fuming like a volcano about to erupt.

Every so often, Delbert looked up to his left to see what Toad was doing. Toad was riding back and forth, very close to the timber, hunching low over the saddle at times, venturing into the brush every so often and wiping his rifle barrel over the tops of bushes. As if he were hunting a rat, Felicity thought.

The herd began to swell. The slowness of the drive allowed the cattle to graze, and none of them got spooked or tried to break ranks with any major attempt. The men worked methodically, pushing the cows southward to the ford across the creek. When a cow did break ranks, Wicks or Smoot or one of the others quickly hazed it back into the herd, uttering only soft, gruff words to back their play.

"Take a look at your homes, gals," Delbert said, toward the end of the drive. "It's probably the last time you'll ever see them."

"Where are you taking us?" Felicity demanded.

"Oh, I've got a place for you, never worry about that. You might come to like it."

"Never," Felicity spat, and Pilar gave her a look of gratitude.

"Never's a hell of a long time, lady," Delbert said.

"Not long enough for you once my husband gets back. He'll hang your sorry hide to the highest tree."

"Big words for a little lady who ain't got no choice. Your man comes after me, I'll gut him like a fish."

Delbert tapped on the handle of a big Bowie knife he carried on his belt.

Felicity didn't say anything. Del was not only a common thief, he was a heartless killer. She looked at Pilar, with what she hoped was encouragement, but Pilar was looking back at the bunkhouses, the Storm's house, the barn. There was a sad look in her eyes. Felicity wondered what she was thinking and wished she could give her some comfort.

The men bunched up the cattle and held them prior to fording the creek. Smoot rode back from the vanguard and spoke to Delbert.

"Want us to run 'em acrost, Del?"

"Yeah, but you stay here. Hiram will give the order."

"Whatcha want me to do, boss?"

"I want you to ride back there and get Toad. If he ain't found that Mex yet, he ain't goin' to."

"Okay."

"Then, Ridley, I want you and Toad to burn them houses and that barn clean down."

"That's what you want us to do, boss?"

"Burn 'em," Delbert said, and Felicity saw the strangest look in his eyes. It was a look of enjoyment and satisfaction, as well as a look of pure lust, almost as if he were bedding an unwilling woman and getting great pleasure from it. Pilar saw the look, too, and winced as if he was looking directly into her eyes.

"Burn 'em to the ground, Ridley," Delbert called after Smoot, who was already riding toward Tod Sutphen.

"I wanna see smoke, you hear?"

Ridley raised his hand and nodded. Then he put the spurs to his horse's flanks and galloped toward the houses.

Hiram rode to the head of the herd and gave the order.

The cattle began to cross the creek, splashing through the shallows, some trying to drink, others prodding the slow ones with their horns.

Felicity saw her life flowing away, everything she and Brad had worked for, leaking out of the pasture toward some unknown destination.

Pilar said something that Felicity could barely hear. But it chilled her blood and made her want to cry.

"*Mi casa,*" Pilar whispered. "My home."

NINETEEN

෧

When Carlos saw the man ride up to the barn, he knew it meant trouble.

He knew it wasn't Brad or Julio.

He knew it was a man he had never seen before. And the man had a rifle, and he looked like he was ready to shoot.

Carlos dropped the bridle in his hand and ran out through the back doors of the barn, shoving one door open just wide enough for him to escape. He ran, and he kept running into the timber. He cursed himself for not strapping on his pistol that morning. And his rifle was still in the bunkhouse. He was defenseless.

He ran because he knew his life depended on it.

When he got to the woods, he kept on running and then he started looking for a place to hide. He stopped when he came to an old well site that hadn't panned out, a depression in the earth that was now overgrown with scrub brush, blackberries, sumac, and alder. Thick brush. He stepped down into the shallow hole, and started pulling dirt and pine needles down into it so that it covered his legs and chest.

He took off his hat, crumpled it up, and put it beneath him. Then he smeared dirt on his face and held his breath for several seconds until his pulse stopped racing.

Later, Carlos heard screams. A woman's screams. But he did not know if the screams were from Pilar or Felicity. The sound sent shivers up his spine. He heard a gunshot, muffled, probably coming from inside the bunkhouse or from the house where Felicity lived.

There were voices. Men's voices and the sound of hoof-beats. Then a long silence, fragments of conversation, words floating up through the timber, distorted fragments that made no sense. And the crunch of iron hooves on small sticks and stones. A man on horseback riding along the fringe of trees just below him. Baffling. Unnerving. Carlos held his breath often. To listen. Trying to decipher what the sounds meant.

The lowing of cattle, the soft breeze through the trees. The muffled voices of men. And the horse, walking along, back and forth, slow and methodical. The rustle of brush, the sudden glint of sunlight shooting through the trees, vanishing like will-o'-the-wisp. The nothingness of nothing. The silences and the low moans of cattle on the move.

It didn't take Carlos long to figure it out. The cattle belonging to Brad Storm were being rustled, being driven from the valley toward the south. And still, the rider waited, riding back and forth, slow and steady. He pictured him. A rider with a gun, watching, looking for Carlos. But not coming into the timber, not in any hurry. Watching and waiting. Looking for him.

He was a rabbit, hiding in a hole. A rabbit with fear and a twitching nose for a mind. *Un conejo*. And much fear. *Mucho miedo*.

He thought in both English and Spanish, and he did not want to die. He did not want to be shot down like a rabbit and left for the buzzards.

Carlos began to tremble. At first the shaking was inside. Then it quivered to his skin and to his hands and legs. He was shivering as if it were winter and there was snow on the ground, frost in the wind. He could not stop shivering.

He could not stop shaking until he felt the first sting on his arm. Then he felt another on his neck. He looked down and saw them. Ants. They were crawling all over his arms, up his sleeve, and onto his neck. Then he saw the anthill, a foot or two from the sunken earth where he was hiding. Hundreds of red ants were streaming toward him, their tiny antennae twitching, their little legs pumping. He slapped at the ants on his arm, batted those on his neck, and got more bites for his trouble.

Carlos scrambled from the hole and felt stings on his crotch and belly. He was crawling with ants, and the stings were like poison needles in his skin. He slapped and brushed, clearing the ants from his trousers, off his arms, and from around his neck. He hopped away from the anthill and waddled to a large pine. He leaned against it and dropped his trousers. He began to pick ants off his body, felt a sting on his ankles. He removed his boots and socks, shook them out. Ants tumbled from his boots and off his socks.

He mashed some of them that were on his body, flicked others away until he was satisfied that he was free of the stinging creatures. He pulled his pants up, sat down and donned his socks, and pulled on his boots. He brushed himself all over, then looked through the trees.

He saw the man patrolling the strip of land just below the woods. He did have a rifle and it was straight up, the buttstock anchored to his ham hock of a leg. He wore a pistol and a cartridge belt, too. He was peering into the trees, looking for any sign of movement.

Carlos knew that as long as he stood still, he was not likely to be seen. He touched his head and realized that he had left his hat in the hole where he had been hiding. He felt naked without it, but he knew he dared not move to retrieve it. He turned his head slightly, hugging tight against the pine tree. He must not move.

It seemed to Carlos that he stood that way, unmoving, for hours. His legs ached, his neck was stiff. And the stings still hurt and began to itch. He knew he could not scratch those places where he had been bitten, and it was torture to just stand there as the poison seeped into his flesh, his veins. Small as the bites were, they were annoying. Maddening at times. He ached to scratch the itching places, but he stood there, knowing his life depended on it.

The man on horseback rode on, up the line and back, disturbing the bushes, stopping to look at something suspicious, slowing his horse every few yards. Looking, looking, always looking. Carlos cringed as one of the ant bites on his neck flared and stung again, then began to itch as if something unseen was burrowing into his flesh.

Then he felt the thirst. His throat began to dry out until it was parched. He felt hot all over his body. He felt sick to his stomach. But there was nothing in it. He had not eaten, nor taken coffee. He was empty and drying out. He licked his lips, and there was very little saliva. He wanted to stoop down and find a small pebble to put in his mouth. That would help take away the thirst. But he could not move. He would not move.

Then, after what seemed like hours, like an eternity, he heard voices.

It took him a moment, but Carlos realized they were calling out to the man who was hunting for him.

"Toad, come on down," one of the men shouted.

"Ain't found him yet."

"Let it go. We're going to burn down the whole shebang."

"Whooeee," Toad yelled, and Carlos saw his horse blur by him, then show his rump as it galloped down the slope toward the barn and dwellings.

"*Mierda*," Carlos said, and scratched his neck, legs, and belly.

He walked slowly down to the edge of the timber and stood behind a tree that shielded his entire body. He peeked out and watched the stalking man ride down to the barn and dismount.

Two other men were just walking into the barn. The

one called Toad entered the barn behind them. Several moments passed by, and then Carlos saw a thin plume of smoke rising from the hayloft window. Smoke leaked from the roof, spewing out from beneath the eaves on the three sides he could see. The three men emerged from the barn carrying torches. One was carrying a shovel, another a rake, and the third a bucket full of flames.

They ran down to his bunkhouse, and the one with the bucket opened the door and threw the entire bucket inside. The other two split off. One ran to Julio's bunkhouse, the last one dashed to the main house. Soon, there was smoke rising from each of the dwellings. The three men mounted their horses and rode off toward the creek.

Carlos looked at the long valley. There was not a single head of cattle to be seen. The pasture was empty of all life. He saw dust rising from across the creek, and then he ran down to the well and pulled up a bucket of sloshing water, untied the rope, and lugged it to the main house. He opened the front door and flames leaped out at him. He threw the water through the doorway straight into the fiery wall that was just beyond the entrance.

The water hissed and went out, having no effect on the flames. Carlos backed off the porch and ran back to the well. By then, both bunkhouses were smoking, and fire was crawling through cracks and climbing the outside walls. The roofs caught on fire. He threw the bucket down beside the well, knowing it was hopeless. All he could do was watch the houses burn.

He did not know whether the fire generated the wind or if the wind came out of the high peaks and fanned the flames, but the fires whipped and lashed the houses, and Carlos watched them crumble one by one, until only the brick chimneys were standing. Smoke filled the air and rose up high in the sky in black and white columns. Then the wind died down and the smoky spires seemed to hang in the air as if they were made of granite. It was a horrible sight to see, and Carlos almost broke into tears.

He stood there, covered with soot and ashes, his face

smeared with dirt, his skin pocked with ant bites, and looked down at his boots and his trousers.

This was all he had in the world now, just the clothes on his back.

Then, he remembered his hat, up in the timber, in that miserable hole where the ants swarmed.

He walked slowly up the slope and into the timber.

His hat was covered with red ants. He reached down and gingerly picked up the crushed remains of his hat. He shook all the ants off, slapped the felt against his trouser legs. When he was satisfied that he had gotten all the ants off, he tried to get the crown back in shape. When he smoothed it, he put his hat on, squared it up, and walked back down to the smoldering buildings.

It was then that Carlos wept.

TWENTY

❧

Brad and Julio broke camp at dawn, when the sky was a pale wash of blue and all the stars were gone. The moon was a skeletal ghost hanging desolate in the far reaches of the horizon like some remnant of a distant world.

"You are pushing it, Brad," Julio said, rising from his bedroll. "The horses are tired. I am tired. Do we break our fast this morning?"

Brad knew he was pushing it. They hadn't had breakfast since they left the Arapaho village, and they had chewed on hardtack and stale jerky the past two days. The horses were tired, and so was he. But he missed Felicity and wanted to get back home. There was that matter of horse tracks down by the creek. And just Pilar, Felicity, and Carlos to keep an eye on things.

"No, Julio. We can be home by noon if we don't dawdle."

"It will be there a half hour after the noon."

"Shake a leg. Ginger's already under saddle."

Julio stood up and stretched. Brad was standing next to his horse, feeding the gelding grain out of his hand. Every bone in Julio's body ached after sleeping on the hard ground two nights in a row, and his stomach was pressing against his backbone. He rolled up his blanket after shaking it out, tied it to the back of his saddle. He picked up the saddle blanket and lay it on Chato's back. He swung the saddle up and bent over to grab a cinch strap. He squared the saddle atop the blanket and began hitching up, trying to ignore the gnawing in his stomach, the desire for coffee strong enough to open his eyes and keep them open.

Brad climbed aboard Ginger and waited for Julio to finish cinching up, slide his rifle back in its boot. Brad flexed his arms and pumped his legs up and down in the stirrups. He, too, was stiff and sore, and wanted coffee, eggs, bacon, anything that Felicity might cook. But they did not have far to go, and he could wait for a hot, sit-down meal with the woman he loved. And missed dearly.

He touched the bulge in his belt. The gold. At least he could make her eyes light up with the dust. That was the only reason he had gone and left her.

But he vowed he would never leave her again for so long a ride.

They rode into the dawn with its peach and salmon sky, gilded clouds, and fresh snowy air blown down from the high ermine-capped peaks. Brad found renewed energy in the morning and zest for the coming day. Ginger's every stride was bringing him closer to home.

"What do you think that old Arapaho brave meant when he said to you that you had 'shoot in your eyes,' Brad?" Julio said.

"I don't know," Brad said.

"I do."

"Yeah? What was that?"

"I have seen that look before. When you drew your pistol and cocked it, you were ready to kill that brave."

"Maybe."

"Ah, no maybe about it," Julio said. "That man was a centimeter from death."

"It was close."

"I saw the look. The 'shoot' look. You had it when that brown bear mauled one of the newborn calves last spring, remember?"

"I remember. Close call for the calf."

"You tried to chase the bear away."

"I tried."

"Then the bear came at you. You drew your pistol. Like lightning. And I saw that look. I think the bear saw it, too."

"The bear kept coming," Brad said.

"And you shot it. Right between the eyes. The bear fell right where you stood."

"Lucky shot."

"There is luck, yes," Julio said. "And skill. And that shoot look I saw in your eyes. Gave me the chilblains."

"I had to shoot the bear."

"You might have had to shoot the Arapaho, too."

"More luck for the brave."

"And for me. They would have shot arrows into our hearts I think."

"Julio, you think too damned much sometimes."

"To think is good, is it not?"

Brad laughed.

"Sometimes," he admitted.

The land looked different now than it had on the drive. Brad saw the same landmarks, but from a different perspective. It seemed he had never ridden this way before, at times, but he was sure of the trail. As he rode, he figured backward, estimating the time it would take to get back home. He chewed on hardtack and stale jerky to stop the rumbling in his stomach. He looked at the fair sky and saw nothing but blue and the white of clouds. Rabbits broke cover and hawks plied the sky looking for small rodents or quail. He heard them cry, their high-pitched whistles piercing the air, and there were quail calling out danger when the hawk's shadow passed over them.

Brad smelled woodsmoke a few minutes before he saw

it. He and Julio were on the last stages of their return journey when the smell wafted through the trees and assailed his nostrils, stinging the membrane inside his nose, descending into his throat and choking him.

"Smell that?" Brad said to Julio.

Julio lifted his drooping head slightly and sniffed, crinkling his nose. He had been dozing, so tired he cared little where they were or how far they had to go.

"Smells like smoke," he said.

"Woodsmoke."

"Yes, that is what I smell."

Brad and Julio, both, like anyone who had lived in the mountains for a time, were very wary of fire. So many timber fires had been started by a streak of lightning or careless hunters. Brad had seen hundreds of acres of pine and other trees ravaged by forest fires so that he was always on the lookout for the telltale signs. Yet, they had had no rain for a week or so. The sky was clear of rain clouds.

He looked up at the sky now, though, and saw what looked like a faint wisp of smoke.

"See that, Julio?" He pointed to the sky.

"Smoke?"

"Looks like."

"Near the ranch, I think."

"Too damned near. Let's see if these horses have any steam left in their boilers."

He tickled Ginger's flanks with his spurs. Julio did the same. The horses were tired, but they responded to the prodding and broke into a trot. Then, with further tickles from the men's spurs, the horses began to lope, then broke into a lazy gallop.

The smell of smoke grew stronger the closer they rode to the ranch. Brad looked up again and saw more smoke, a black scrawl of it just above the pine trees. Then, the closer he got to the valley pasture, the thicker and blacker the smoke.

He was not prepared for what he saw when he rounded the bend and came upon the valley. There he saw an empty pasture and smoke rising from the two bunkhouses, the barn, and his own home.

He felt something plummet in his chest. Julio cried out: "*Ay de mi*," and his voice was full of anguish and a pain that was not from any wound, but from some deep place in his heart, a place of profound sorrow.

"What the hell," Brad said, and rode straight for his burning house.

Only the chimney was standing when he reined up Ginger, and he felt an unseen hand tighten on his throat. The first thing he thought of was Felicity being in that house, burned to a crisp, and as his throat tightened, tears welled up in his eyes and he crumpled in the saddle, wracked with grief.

The floor had not yet burned through, but all else was gone. He saw the topsy-turvy shape of the woodstove in what had been the kitchen, the melted and mangled wreckage of pots and pans, the twisted copper of something unrecognizable, the singed and fluttering remnants of papers he had kept in a strongbox. And, beneath the house, something smoking, something he should have recognized but didn't. It could have been Felicity herself, all charred and smoking. He saw a fluttering of hair, and his insides twisted into a wrenching knotted clump that made him want to vomit.

Julio rode by, heading for his bunkhouse. Brad looked up and saw Carlos running toward him from the well, an empty wooden bucket in his hand. His face was covered with soot and dirt. He looked as if he had crawled out of a hole in the depths of the earth. His pants were dirty, too, and his hat looked as if it had been crushed by a steam piledriver. All crumpled and misshapen, the hat's felt crown smashed and smeared with dirt.

"Carlos," Brad called out, "what happened here?"

"They come," Carlos said, panting as he came to a stop. He dropped the bucket, and it clattered woodenly as it rolled a foot or two. "They steal the cattle. They burn the barn and the houses."

"What about Felicity? And Pilar?"

"They take them. The men take them and all the cattle."

Julio turned his horse and rode back to where Carlos and Brad were talking.

"Where is Pilar?" he asked, his voice squeaking from a tight throat.

"She is gone, too, Julio," Carlos said. "The men, they take her and Felicity."

"Who were they?" Brad asked.

"I do not know."

"How come you're still here? Where were you when the men came?"

Carlos explained that he had been in the barn and ran into the timber.

"The man who hunts me is called Toad. I think they steal my horse, too. I . . . my guns . . . they are in the bunkhouse. I am looking for them. I could do nothing, Brad."

"They rustled my cattle, they stole our women, why in hell did they burn down our houses?"

He was not expecting an answer. He was just voicing his own puzzlement over such a tragedy. But Carlos answered him anyway.

"They are very bad men," he said. "They want to kill, and they want to hurt. Toad hunted me. Only to shoot me. They did not have to burn down our homes. They did not have to do that."

Brad looked over at his house. He was relieved that Felicity was alive, but he was sick inside knowing that she was with several men.

"What is that under my house, Carlos? It has hair and could be human."

"Oh, no, it is not human," Carlos said. "I think it is your dog. I heard a shot before they . . . before . . ."

"Before they took Felicity and Pilar?" Brad said.

"Yes. I think they shot Curly. I think that is Curly under your house."

Brad was sick again. Over the dog. The dog that loved

them. The dog that they loved. He must have been trying to protect Felicity when they shot him. Or Curly was just trying to be friendly, maybe jumping up on one of the men.

The dog must have been easy to kill. Just one shot.

"I am sorry, Brad," Carlos said.

Julio was crying. He did not try to wipe away his tears; he just sat slumped in his saddle, sobbing. He looked like a beaten man.

"How many men came here?" Brad asked, swinging down out of the saddle.

"I do not know. I saw three. But there were more, I know. Some of them were driving the cattle when three others started the fires. The barn burned very fast and so did the houses. The men rode off and all the cattle are gone."

"Would you recognize those three men if you saw them again?" Brad asked.

"I would recognize Toad. The other two were far away. Why?"

Brad looked around at the ruins of what had once been a ranch. Now, it was only a smoldering ruin. He thought of the Seguin house. His own would look like that, in time. It was such a terrible loss, and the rustlers had two good and innocent women with them. The men had to be caught and punished.

Julio dismounted. He walked over and hugged Carlos. Then he turned to Brad and stretched out his arms. The two men hugged each other.

"We'll get them, Julio," Brad said. "I promise. We'll get Pilar and Felicity back."

Julio could not stop sobbing.

"We will get them," Carlos said. "I want to hang them. I want them to die slow."

"I—I want them, too," Julio said, sniffling and wiping his face with the back of his sleeve. "I want them to die slow, too. For taking Pilar and Felicity. For shooting Curly and for poisoning our dogs."

"And the cattle," Carlos said.

"The cattle be damned," Brad said. "I want those men to dance with lead in their gullets. I want to see their blood wet and red on the ground."

Julio looked at him. It was a sharp, perceptive look.

"There it is," he said, softly.

'What?" Brad said, doubling up his fist with a repressed anger.

"You have shoot in your eyes, Brad."

Brad heaved a long breath. His nostrils flared.

"You're damned right I do," he said.

And the smoke stung his eyes, but that is not what made him cry just then.

He thought of what those men might do to his wife and Julio's. There was no time to waste. He must track them and find them and get the women away from them.

And kill them, each man, one by one.

TWENTY-ONE

❧

Delbert Coombs knew he might not have much time to drive the herd to its destinations. He had the men drive the cattle back into the creek and wade part of it. He crossed the stream four times before he issued further orders.

"This is where we split the herd up," he told Ridley Smoot. "First, we do some horse swapping." He turned to look at Felicity and Pilar. "We're goin' to swap horses with you gals."

"What?" Felicity said.

"You heard me. Ridley, help the little lady off her horse."

Ridley dismounted and helped Felicity dismount. He pulled her from the saddle and stood her up straight. She struggled with her bonds, but they didn't give.

Pilar did not own a horse and wasn't comfortable riding. She was on Carlos's horse, Tico. Toad helped her out of the saddle. She fell into his arms, cried out in pain when her arm twisted as she tried to maintain her balance with her hands tied behind her back.

"Ridley, you ride that bobtailed Arab. Give your horse to the Mexican gal."

"She ain't no rider, Del."

"Well, she ain't goin' far," Del said.

Tod Sutphen helped Pilar up on Ridley's horse, which stood nearly fifteen hands high, about the same height as Tico, coal black with one white stocking and a small blaze on its forehead.

"Horse's name is Choc," Ridley said. "Short for chocolate."

Pilar said nothing as she sat in the saddle, looking lost and bewildered. Felicity patted her leg to reassure her.

"Toad, you swap horses with Mrs. Storm here."

Toad rode up on his sturdy gelding, a steeldust gray with a good deep chest, fine bone structure, standing better than fifteen hands high.

"You take good care of Mouse," he told Felicity. "I put a lot of store in him."

Felicity said nothing. She just glared at Toad, a glare that was mingled with open revulsion. He took her reins and handed her his.

"Help her up on that horse, Ridley."

She glared at him, too.

"Now, Toad, you and Fred cut out seventy-five head and drive them to the stockyards we set up down toward Granite."

"We can make that in no time, boss," Toad said. "You want us to start butcherin'?"

"There are at least a half dozen butchers standing by there. Dale Creed's in charge. You tell him to cut 'em up and pack 'em real quick."

"You got it, Del."

Toad and Fred Raskin began cutting the herd while Delbert spoke to Ridley and Abner Wicks.

"You boys cut out another seventy or so head and drive 'em to the stockyards we set up at Rusty's camp. You know the place."

"We know it well, boss," Ridley said. "Rusty'll be there?"

"Yeah, tell him to start butcherin'. You and Abner help

him pack the meat and load the wagons. Wait for word on the delivery."

"Sure," Ridley said. "I cut meat for Rusty Crabb when he was legitimate."

The men all laughed.

"Hiram, you and I will take the women and drive the few remaining head down to the yards outside Oro City. That's a pretty safe place, and we won't leave a lot of tracks."

"Might have fifty head when the boys get through cuttin'," Hiram said.

"I have orders for those fifty head, and I mean to deliver by week's end."

"We can do 'er," Hiram said.

Delbert rode away to talk to the others one more time as they were thinning the herd into three columns.

"Wipe out all your tracks," he told each man. "Make sure you cut off the marked ears and burn 'em once you get to the yards."

"You think somebody's comin' after us, Del?" Toad asked.

"You never know. Count on it."

"Will do," Toad said, as did all the others who got their final orders.

Delbert and Hiram, along with Felicity and Pilar, continued driving fifty head of cattle down the creek. Then they cut north over preselected ground, hardpan that left few tracks, a place where a mountain had been ground down to powder eons in the past, and over the years, water, wind, and roaming game herds had flattened the terrain further.

Delbert was a careful man, a planner, and he had long ago set up isolated and secluded stock pens and abattoirs, secured the services of butchers, some old mountain men, others drunkards and wastrels who had lived off the land for years. These were his butchers, and he paid them well.

For some years he had been stealing cattle from unsuspecting ranchers, butchering them, and selling them to restaurants or hash houses, mostly in the mining towns where the proprietors didn't ask too many questions. He had a smooth, solid operation because of his policy of secrecy. His men were all handpicked and efficient. They weren't hesitant about killing, and none had any qualms about rustling cattle. In fact, every man jack among 'em was a criminal, just like Del and his brother, Hiram.

"You gals come with Hiram and me," Delbert said to Felicity. "And, maybe, I better know your names before we start out. How about you, Mrs. Storm? You got a name."

"I wouldn't have it on your filthy lips," Felicity said.

Delbert laughed, but it was not a humorous laugh. Rather it was full of derision. That told Felicity a lot. Delbert had no more feelings for her than he did for Curly. And she was likely to suffer a similar fate, she believed.

"How about you, little Mexican gal? You got a name."

Pilar looked at Felicity, a questioning glint in her eyes.

"I am called Pilar," she said, meekly. "And my friend is Felicity."

Felicity gave Pilar a sympathetic look. She wasn't angry at her. Pilar just didn't want any trouble with these rough, crude men; that was all. Felicity didn't blame her. But at least she hadn't told Delbert her name.

"Pretty names," Delbert said. "Pretty ladies to boot. Let's move out. Hiram, you take Pilar with you. She tries to run off, shoot her dead. Felicity, you stick close to me, so's you and me can get more acquainted."

Felicity held her tongue for the moment. Delbert gave her a scornful look, and she turned her head away from him. She wasn't going to give this man an inch, she told herself. He'd soon take a mile.

The other two herds disappeared after a few moments. Hiram and Delbert moved their small herd in a different direction, heading north. They crossed the creek again and wound through scrub pines, hugged the rimrock before dropping down on an ancient moraine that had been ground down over the years. It was wide and strewn with small pebbles and sand that had once been huge boulders. From the looks of the limestone and the hillocks, a river had once coursed through there and over time, with plenty of raging flash floods, the rocks had been pummeled and crushed and reduced to small chunks, and these had been eroded into the flatness and smallness they now possessed. The cattle left no tracks other than a turned over pebble here and there. The bottoms of these were only slightly damp and would soon dry in the sun. The sun was climbing toward its zenith.

After a time, Delbert no longer looked over his shoulder to see if he was being followed. The moraine had twisted several times, and he felt safe from immediate pursuit.

Felicity watched his every move and made note of their route in case she lived through this and had to remember it later.

She was hot and hungry and powerless to wipe the perspiration off her face. The sun was boiling at that lower altitude.

Delbert slipped the strap of his wooden canteen off his saddle horn, took a few swallows, then held out the vessel to Felicity.

"Want a drink?" he asked.

"I'll drink," she said, "and if you'll be so kind, would you take that bandanna from around your neck and wipe my forehead? The sweat's stinging my eyes."

"Why, sure," Delbert said. He untied his bandanna and leaned over, wiped her forehead. Then he put the canteen to her lips, and tipped it so that water trickled out of it and into her mouth and throat.

"Enough?" he said.

"Yes."

He corked the canteen, slung it from his saddle horn, and stuffed his bandanna in his back pocket after wiping the grime from his neck.

"Delbert? Is that your name?" Felicity said.

"Yeah, but you can call me Del."

"It's Coombs, isn't it?"

"You know my name?"

"I've heard it before," she said.

"Hell, everybody in these parts knows my name. What did you hear about me?"

"That you murdered a family named Seguin and stole all their cattle."

"Don't nobody have no proof of that."

"I have a question for you," she said.

"Go right ahead."

"You stole our cattle. You kidnapped me and my friend Pilar. Why did you have to burn down our houses? Why did you burn our barn?"

"Oh, you been wonderin' about that, have you?"

"I can't help but wonder. There was no reason to do that. You got what you wanted. I'm frankly curious."

"Well, curiosity killed the dadgummed cat, you know. Still, it's probably a fair question."

"Are you going to answer it?"

"I might. Never thought about it real hard. The way I figure it in your case is that your man is off somewhere. Pilar's, too, right?"

"Right. They're probably back by now."

"Well, with the barn gone and the houses burned, they can't get no grub ner any more ammunition. Slow 'em down. I don't like to leave no tracks."

"Brad—my husband—is an excellent tracker."

"He is, is he? Well, now we'll just see how good he is, won't we?"

"We sure will, Mr. Coombs."

"Well, I wouldn't worry about it much. We ain't got far to go, and once these cows smell water, they'll run to where we keep 'em. After that, any trackers will run right into a wall of lead."

"I wouldn't be so damned smug if I were you, Mr. Coombs."

"Oh, you wouldn't, would you? Hell, lady, you know, I just don't give a damn."

"I can see that. Pride goeth before a fall."

"Oh, I've heard that in Sunday school. I still don't give a damn."

She said no more. She had sized up Delbert Coombs pretty well.

He was a heartless, cruel man, with no morals, no conscience. He would murder people and burn their homes down without so much as batting an eye.

Such a man was dangerous.

Now she knew just how dangerous he was.

She thought of Brad and wondered if he could track them. The herd had been split into three separate groups. Which one would he follow? She knew now why Coombs had switched horses. Brad would track her horse, most probably.

Delbert was very cunning, she thought. He may have outwitted Brad.

But, sooner or later, she was sure, Brad would figure it out.

If he did not and followed her horse, he would ride straight into an ambush or arrive at a dead end. It all seemed hopeless now that she thought about it. And she wanted him so much, wanted his arms around her. But she was a hostage, and if Coombs was using her as bait to kill Brad . . .

Well, she didn't know the answer to that question.

She was filled with an overwhelming feeling of dread.

Deep dread.

And a sudden sadness that passed all understanding.

TWENTY-TWO

❧

Brad knew the horses were tired. That last gallop had taken the last of their spunk. They were not lathered yet but were close to it. And two horses were all that the three of them had.

"For want of a horse," he said aloud and to no one.

Julio was still in shock. He stood there, dazed, looking at the burned remnants of his bunkhouse, his wife gone, along with all of his possessions. He stood there, like a man whose arms had been cut off.

"What you say?" Carlos asked.

"Oh, nothing. Just an old phrase about war and the want of a nail."

"I do not understand."

"Let's see if we can find your guns in the bunkhouse, Carlos. Get that bucket, fill it, and we'll douse any of the hot spots."

"That is what I wished to do when you came up. My pistol was under my bed. My rifle . . . I do not remember where my rifle was. Maybe in the kitchen. Maybe by the back door. Maybe it fell outside when . . ."

"We'll see if we can find them," Brad said. He turned to Julio with his tear-streaked face, his red-rimmed eyes, eyes with the haunting look of loss flickering in them like a dim lamp in a fog. "Julio, take care of the horses, will you? Strip them, walk them, see if you can find any unburned grain in the barn. Water them. Give 'em a good rubdown."

He put his hands on Julio's shoulders, squeezed them.

"The way to get over loss, Julio, is to build something, plan something. We'll go after Pilar and Felicity before the sun sets."

"I know," Julio said. "If I keep busy, my heart will not have so much pain."

"That's the idea," Brad said.

Julio led the horses toward the smoking ruins of the barn. Brad walked to the bunkhouse, met Carlos at the well. Brad helped him carry the full bucket of water.

"Let's start looking where you think your pistol might be," Brad said. "Show me where you had your bunk."

Carlos walked around the side of the smoldering frame of the bunkhouse cabin. Tendrils of smoke rose from some of the logs that were still burning in certain places.

"There," he said.

Within the downed walls, Brad saw shards of exploded glass, the blackened remnants of peaches, apricots, and pears, blackberry preserves, and unrecognizable vegetables. Swollen airtights with their labels partially burned away lay helter-skelter in the area that had once been the kitchen. There were knives, spoons, and forks scattered and twisted into grotesque shapes, amid cracked pewter plates, a skillet, and a fry pan, and cracked clay bowls next to burned wooden canisters and bowls.

"Before you pour any water in there, Carlos, get a stick and poke around where you think your pistol might be."

The smoke was making them all sick to their stomachs. It hung in the air like torn shrouds. Brad was coughing. So, too, was Carlos. Carlos returned soon with a long planed one-by-two that they used to measure creek and well water. He began poking in the ashes and charred chunks of logs, stirring the ashes, pushing away clumps of a cotton-stuffed mattress, goose feathers from his pillow, scraps of a woolen blanket, and the melted gobs of a black slicker.

"Take it slow, Carlos. You don't want to stir the small fires."

Poke, poke, poke. Stir, stir, stir.

The end of the wood strip clunked against something metal. Carlos worked it toward the edge of the room, wormed it past the smoking log wall and onto the ground.

"That looks like a pistol," Brad said. "Careful, it's probably hotter'n a branding iron."

Carlos picked up the bucket and poured a small amount of water over the object. Flakes and globs of burned cotton and fragments of feathers washed away. The outlines of a pistol barrel showed, then the trigger, trigger guard, hammer, and butt came into view. The wooden grip was only partially burned on one side. The pistol hissed as it cooled, and a thin mist steamed from the hot metal.

"Maybe we can find some oil, and you can clean it up," Brad said as Carlos gingerly lifted the pistol up by its trigger guard. "It looks okay. Cock it, but don't fire off a bullet if there are any in the cylinder."

"There are five," Carlos said.

"Be careful then."

Carlos turned toward the pasture and thumbed the hammer back. The cylinder spun from an empty tube to one with a cartridge in the chamber. He eased the hammer back down to half cock.

"*Se sirve*," he said in Spanish. "It works."

"Good. Now set it down and let's look for your rifle."

"I do not know where the holster is," Carlos said as they walked around the house. "I take the pistol out at night and put it under my bed."

"Probably burned to a crisp."

They looked over toward the barn. Julio was letting the horses drink at the water trough. They were unsaddled, their wet blankets drying in the sun.

Carlos carried the stick with him, while Brad carried the sloshing bucket of water. They walked around to where the back door used to be, and Carlos began poking through the rubble. The logs in the back had not burned through. They were still standing four high, still hot and still smoking. Brad sloshed water on what was left of the doorjamb. There was a hissing of steam.

Carlos reached around with one hand, feeling for the rifle. It was not there.

"Check the floor," Brad said. "Use the stick."

Carlos leaned in and poked around with the stick. He felt something hard and worked it toward the doorway.

"I think it is there," he said.

"Don't touch it with your hands," Brad said. "It's probably still hot."

Brad poured water onto the object and slowly its outlines began to appear. The rifle, a Winchester '73, like his own, seemed to have suffered no major damage to its barrel or receiver. The stock was scorched but could be sanded and refinished, after which it would be as good as new.

"You can see what you must do for both your pistol and your rifle, Carlos."

"Yes. Much work."

"Well, you are going to have to make do by yourself. Julio and I are going to track those rustlers. I'll buy you another horse in Oro City. In the meantime, you'll have to find a way to feed yourself while we're gone."

"There is no food here."

"Fire doesn't consume everything, my friend. You'll have to go through all the buildings to find what you need. I can give you cartridges for your rifle. You may have to hunt. There is plenty of game in these mountains."

"I will be a rat."

Brad smiled.

"Yes, for a time. You have water. Build yourself a shelter up in the timber. You'll probably find tools. Make do."

"I will," Carlos said.

Brad set the bucket down and looked around at the bunk-houses, his own house, and the barn. Make do, he thought, that's all any of us can do right now. He felt sorry for Carlos, but Carlos could make do for a time, just as Brad would have to do. Carlos could find food and tools to keep him going until Brad and Julio returned with Pilar and Felicity.

Brad walked over to the razed barn and the watering trough.

"Did you find some grain, Julio?" he asked.

"Enough, I think."

"We have to track those cattle as soon as we can."

"I am ready."

"It will be slow. We might have to walk the horses some of the way."

"Yes. They are tired."

"Carlos will have to stay here."

"He can ride with me."

"No. Riding double would wear Chato down too much. He will stay. You and I will go on."

Julio looked toward Carlos and shook his head.

"Maybe you are right."

Brad looked at the horses. He patted Ginger's withers. Ginger whinnied.

"You'll be all right, boy," he said.

"Julio, let's get the horses under saddle. I'm going to give Carlos some .44 cartridges. We'll get him a new horse when we can."

"It is good that you have the gold."

"Yes," Brad said.

They saddled the horses. Brad gave Carlos twenty .44 rifle cartridges, most of what little food they had left, and waved good-bye. He and Julio walked the horses down through the valley, crossed the creek, and then they mounted Ginger and Chato. Julio looked back at the smoking remains of the ranch. Brad did not. What was done, was done, he thought. Looking at the devastated buildings would not bring them back.

Julio muttered something to himself, an epithet or a prayer, Brad wasn't sure which, and a faraway look came into his eyes before he turned his horse. Brad nodded that he understood and looked down at the ground.

"The tracking will be easy," he said.

"Maybe," Julio said.

"They can't move fast."

"Neither can we move fast, *jefe*."

"We can move faster than two hundred head of cattle."

"Where do the rustlers take them?"

"Good question. We'll just have to find out for ourselves."

The two men rode well into the afternoon. Both were hungry. They had filled their canteens, and both had some jerky and hardtack to sustain them until the next day at least.

Brad realized that Coombs and his bunch were already trying to hide their tracks, wading the cattle down the creek at times. But it was difficult to conceal so many cow tracks, not to mention those of the horses.

"Can you make out the hoofprints of Carlos's horse, Julio?" Brad asked as he finished deciphering the different horse tracks.

"No."

"There is a small nick in the shoe on Tico's left hind leg."

"And Rose?"

"That one," Brad said, pointing to a hoofprint that was slightly blurred on the edges. "I was meaning to shoe Felicity's horse when I got around to it. The shoes are worn down. The rustlers' shoes are all pretty new."

"I see it," Julio said.

They walked the horses for a time, rode them slow when they were mounted.

Late in the afternoon, Brad ran into a maze of tracks, each going in different directions.

"Uh oh," he said.

"What is wrong?" Julio asked.

"They split up the herd. Three different directions."

"That is bad."

"Damned bad," Brad said. "Give me a few minutes to figure out which way Pilar and Felicity went."

Brad walked over each set of tracks. It wasn't easy. The three paths were a maze of cattle and horse spoor. It took a lot of time for him to figure out which horses went with each portion of the split-up herd. Julio waited, holding the reins of Brad's horse while he studied the tracks.

Finally, Brad walked back and took his reins from Julio.

"Bad news, Julio."

"Bad news?"

"We're going to have to split up. I don't like it, but that's the way it is."

"Why?"

"Felicity's horse went south with about seventy-some-odd head. Pilar went in a different direction. I'll show you the way."

"This is not good," Julio said.

"No. It means we split our forces. It will be dangerous for you."

"And for you."

"For both of us. But, we can't just give up. Not now."

"No, we do not give up, Brad."

"No telling where they're taking the cattle or our women."

"We do not know, that is true."

"Is this the way you want to do it? You follow Pilar, and I'll follow Felicity?"

"I do not know what to do."

"If we find one, we may lose the other."

"That is true."

"We must plan on meeting after we find our wives."

"Yes. Where?"

"In Oro City. Two sets of tracks, the one where Pilar is, go toward town. I have to get a horse for Carlos."

"Oro City, yes."

"Do you know the cantina, High Grade?"

"Yes. I know it. It is where the miners take their cups."

"Let's give it two days. No matter what. You meet me at the High Grade."

"I will have Pilar with me."

"*Buena suerte*, Julio."

"*Suerte*," Julio said. "Have the luck."

The two men said good-bye and started out on their separate paths.

Soon, Brad was alone, following a track that would dim with the dusk, fade in the dark. Julio would face the same dilemma. They would have to feel their way, ride blind much of the night.

Brad knew only one thing. Felicity rode with two men. If he could catch them off guard, he might have a chance to rescue his wife. That was the thought that kept him going long after the sun set and every bone in his body ached. He hoped the men he tracked would stop for the night and make camp, light a fire, bed the cattle down.

When the moon rose, he knew that he had hoped for too much.

The tracks went on into the darkest night of his life.

TWENTY-THREE

❧

Brad heard the groans and grunts of the cattle long before he saw them. The sounds carried on the night air and they told him some of the story. The cattle were no longer moving. They were bunched up or corralled somewhere to the south of him. From the bellows and moos, he figured they were in a draw or some other tight space, crowded together.

He had no idea what time it was. The moon was high and thin, curved as a snipped-off fingernail, and the stars so close he could almost feel their cold glow on his face. It had turned chill, and he shivered in the light denim jacket he wore over his flannel shirt.

When he looked down at the ground, he saw that it had been dragged clean of tracks. He could barely make out the drag marks, but they were there, as if someone had pulled a wide board across the road. And it was a road; he knew now. How long he had been on a cut road, he didn't know, but it might have been after he crossed a dry streambed that had seemed unusually wide

The darkness played tricks on a man's eyes. Brad knew

that, but he was surprised at himself for not noticing how the land had changed under his feet. He should have noticed the change of sound from his horse's hoofbeats, the subtle change of vegetation. Had his mind wandered? Of course it had, he reasoned. He had thought of Felicity and Pilar and even of Carlos and Julio. They were men who had depended on him, not only for sustenance and jobs, but also for their safety. He had gone off, chasing after gold, and left the ranch at the mercy of rustlers and killers.

Yes, his mind had wandered, and he hadn't realized that he was riding down a road. A man-made road, blasted out of a hill or mountain, graded, widened, flattened.

But now he knew. And he knew it was an old road, built for a purpose. In the starlight and the thin light of the moon, he could make out limestone bluffs off to his right, the talus-strewn ditch, the shards of shale that signified someone had used dynamite to take out a natural obstacle to the road.

He felt imprisoned by that road and the low cliffs. He felt as if he had ridden into a trap and mentally kicked himself for being a fool who had lost sight of his objective. Sure, he was tired, but he was also burning inside. Burning to rescue his wife, burning for vengeance, and sick at the loss of his home and his cattle. And Felicity.

He stopped for a moment and blinked his eyes several times to see if his night vision could be sharpened. He looked at trees and tried to find definition. He looked at the sky and then at the ground. Was that a bush or a man? Was that a cactus growing beside the road or a man lying on the ground with a rifle in his hands?

He could smell the cattle now. He could smell their offal and their hides. Now that he looked at the ground more carefully, he could see their cow pies swept to the ditch by some kind of wooden or metal drag. And, when he leaned down so his eyes were closer to the ground, he could make out a faint track or two of a horse or a cow.

How far away were the cattle? He did not know. Half a mile? A mile? Two? Hard to tell. But he could smell them, and if he could smell them, they were not far. And two men and a woman, his woman, would be with them.

He must be careful now. He knew that. The road ahead curved, and it might be a perfect place for an ambush. A man could sit there, behind a rock or a tree, and shoot Brad as he rounded the bend.

It seemed to get darker, and Brad knew he would be making a huge mistake to keep blindly riding down that man-made road. Despite his eagerness to rescue Felicity, he knew he had to stop, wait for daylight.

Or almost daylight.

If he was going to be of any help to Felicity, he had to be able to see.

Brad turned Ginger around and began looking for a place to bed down for the night. He rode back until he ran out of bluff and saw trees, a place to get off the road and hide out for the night. Get some rest. Rest Ginger.

He found such a place, and he marked his bearings when he left the road, making sure it was the road and not the wide streambed. He rocked in the saddle as Ginger climbed into the timber. On a level place, he took his bearings from the North Star. He would need to sleep facing east, so the first flicker of sun would wake him. He took his time looking for a suitable spot to lay out his bedroll and sleep until dawn.

And there was such a place on a small shelf of rimrock. A place where he could hobble Ginger on grass and be high enough so that he could look down on anyone who might approach during the night.

He left Ginger saddled, hobbled him, and climbed up onto the ledge, carrying his bedroll and rifle, his canteen and saddlebags. He walked up and down the rocky outcropping to make sure it was clear of snakes and scorpions. He laid out his bedroll, placed his saddlebags at one end. He used one of them, the softest, for a pillow and lay down. He pulled his wool blanket over him, set his pistol within reach under the unused saddlebag.

Ginger was quiet, grazing. If anyone tried to come up

to where Brad was, the horse would whicker or whinny to warn him. He closed his eyes and felt the tiredness begin to seep from his legs and bones. A fresh breeze tugged at his hat, and he took it off, put small rocks on the brim. He lay back down and closed his eyes again.

He fell asleep, dreaming of golden rivers and green pastures, of a woman like Felicity running across a glacier field with wolves chasing her, and of a rifle in his hands that would not work, its mechanism falling apart, spilling to the ground as he ran through hard-rock canyons and over windswept hillocks crawling with spiders and snakes.

Brad awoke just before dawn as if he had an alarm clock in his brain. One moment he was sound asleep, and the next his eyes opened and the tips of the pines came into sharp focus. It was still dark, but he could see the sky becoming just a tinge lighter as if the blackness was slowly bleeding away with the first light of the unseen sun.

He grabbed his hat, plunked it on his head, pulled his pistol from under the saddlebag, holstered it, and walked off into the woods to relieve himself. He stretched his arms, yawned away the last dregs of sleepiness, rolled up his bed, hefted his saddlebags, rifle, and canteen, and slid on his butt the short way to the flat where Ginger lifted his head and nickered to him softly.

He slid his Winchester back in its sheath, set the saddlebags atop Ginger's rump, and took a swallow of water before slinging his canteen onto his saddle horn and pulling himself up into the saddle.

He was hungry, but he was not going to eat. He never ate before he went hunting. He told Felicity that fasting sharpened his senses. He could see and smell game better on an empty stomach.

He rode back down to the road. The sky was slowly paling and just before Ginger stepped onto the road, he saw a glimmer of cream spreading across the eastern sky, prying open the night. The stars faded into pale blue, and the sliver of moon was all but a memory as he went up the road. With each freshening of the light, he studied the ground. It was as he had suspected the night before, some-one had dragged the road to obliterate all the horse and cow tracks.

Now he smelled them again as he climbed a shallow grade. At the top, the smell was much stronger. Lots of cattle leave lots of waste, especially if they are in a con-fined space, such as a corral or a tight gather. The sky blazed in the east, spawning bright splotches of gold and russet on the long pennants of clouds drifting high above the horizon, and he could hear jays, the throaty cooing of doves, and a far-off quail. And the bawling of cattle, deep rumbling in dozens of throats, like the sound of hungry bulls kept from pasture.

He found a place to ground-tie Ginger. He left his rifle in its scabbard, pulled his pistol, and spun the cylinder. Six bullets and half a box of cartridges were on his belt. It would be close work, he thought. Pistol work. So, no rifle.

He walked down below the road through a swale of tall weeds, rocks, and stagnant pools of water, jiggling with insects. Cockleburs clung to the cuffs of his trousers, and his boots crunched lightly on gravel. Water drained through this ditch, he thought, and with the cattle lowing, nobody was likely to hear him.

The road curved, and then he saw the pens. To his amazement, there were cattle crammed into an elaborate array of fencing that formed a stockyard. Beyond were two or three long buildings, with lofts and open windows. One small building behind them looked like a dwelling for a bunkhouse. Smoke rose from its chimney, and he could smell food cooking.

The cattle were squeezed tight together and protesting. A line of wagons, maybe a dozen of them, stood around the compound.

He walked past the stockyards and crept up to the build-ing where he could hear low voices and smell the heady aroma of fresh-brewed coffee. There were no men out-side. He detected at least four voices, all pitched differently. He crept up to a window, pistol in hand, and slowly raised his head to peer inside.

The window was slightly steamed, but he could see inside the room. It looked like a combination office, bunkhouse, and cookshack. Just one big room, with a desk, a table, bunks along at least two walls, chairs, a stove, sideboards. A coffeepot burbled and steamed. Men sitting around the table, smoking, drinking coffee. One old man with white sideburns was pushing a spatula around in a large skillet, and Brad could smell biscuits rising in the oven.

"Toad," one man said, "you better give me a head count afore we start butcherin'. I want pay for every head I saw up."

"After I get some vittles in my belly, Cap," Toad said, and Brad knew that Toad had to be one of the rustlers. But where was Felicity? He looked at every corner he could see and at all the bunks. There was no Felicity.

Brad waited. He waited while the men ate, and when some went to the outhouse out back, he looked them over. Four of them were wearing leather aprons. Two were not. Toad and another man.

There was a corral beyond the outhouse he hadn't noticed before. He sneaked past the bunkhouse and looked at the horses eating grain from a trough or drinking at the small tank.

And then he saw the two horses that were tied up and still saddled. One of them was Rose, Felicity's horse, who stood hipshot. Rose raised her head when she saw him and nickered softly.

Damn, Brad thought, Felicity's here.

Or is she?

Had he been tricked? Had one of the rustlers swapped horses with her just to throw him off track?

Brad's jaw hardened, and his eyes slitted with anger. Where was she?

He walked back to a place of concealment near the stock pens and waited. He holstered his pistol but kept his hand close to its butt.

Finally, he saw Toad and another man walking toward the pens. The other man carried a tablet and pencil.

"I call 'em and you tally 'em, Freddie," Toad said. "Let's get it over with."

"Can you even count, Toad?"

"I sure as hell can count fists poundin' your face to mush if you don't shut your smart mouth, Freddie."

"Aw, I was just a-joshin'."

Toad was puffing on a cheroot. Freddie was spitting tobacco juice. Neither man was looking in Brad's direction when he drew his pistol and stepped in front of them. He pulled his rattles out with his left hand and shook them.

Both men stopped in their tracks.

"What the hell . . ." Toad said.

Then he heard the click of the Colt in Brad's hand as he cocked the trigger.

"Sweet Jesus," Freddie said.

"Who in hell are you?" Toad demanded, jerking the cheroot from his mouth.

"They call me Sidewinder," Brad said, and shook the rattles again.

He watched both men as the color drained from their faces.

Then he stopped rattling, and it was silent.

It was silent for a long time, it seemed.

When a man faces death, that last second can seem like an eternity. And an eternity can seem like the single tick of a doomsday clock.

TWENTY-FOUR

In the singular moment when no man breathed, Brad fixed his eyes on the man called Toad.

"That bay mare one of you rode in here. It belongs to my wife. Now, I want to know one thing, Toad. Where is she?"

Toad took his gaze away from the rattles in Brad's left hand. He looked at the cocked .45, its barrel so close it made him ooze sweat as if he were a sieve.

"She ain't here," he said.

"You didn't answer my question, Toad."

Toad looked at Raskin. Raskin licked dry lips.

"You ain't goin' to shoot us, are you?" Fred Raskin said.

"If I don't get the answer I want."

"Jeez," Raskin said.

"You keep your trap shut, Freddie," Toad said.

"I don't aim to get kilt over'n a danged woman," Raskin said.

"It's up to you, Toad," Brad said. "First the balls, then square between your sorry eyes."

Brad lowered the gun barrel to aim at Toad's crotch. Toad's sweating increased until his palms were oily.

"I don't know," Toad said. "Boss took her and the Mexican gal with him."

"Who's your boss?"

"Delbert Coombs," Raskin blurted out. "He's the one what's got them wimmin."

"And where is Coombs?" Brad asked.

"I dunno," Toad said. "Honest."

"Honest? Hell, you don't know the meaning of the word," Brad said. "Either I get an answer, or I'll blow both of you to hell. Those are my cattle you've got in these pens, and that's a hanging offense."

"Mister," Toad said, "Del Coombs took them wimmin, and I don't know where."

"Toward Oro City," Raskin said. He was shaking now. His knees jiggled inside his trousers. He looked like a turpentined cat, and his face was almost sheet white.

"That true, Toad?"

"I reckon."

"You point me there, and you can walk out of here, both of you."

"He's got a place north of town, and in Oro City, he stays at the best hotel," Raskin said.

"You little bastard," Toad growled. But he was still sweating like an eight-furlong horse.

"You," Brad said to Fred, "drop your gunbelt. Run and fetch me that bay mare back there. Be quick about it, and keep your mouth shut."

Raskin put his tablet and pencil on the ground, then unbuckled his belt and let his pistol and holster drop to the ground. He turned and trotted back to the stables, his boot heels making him wobble like a wheel out of round.

"You ain't got a chance against Del Coombs," Toad said, licking his dry lips.

"I've got a little advice for you, Toad," Brad said. "These are stolen cattle. If they're not back on my ranch by week's end, I'll come gunning for you. Just you. You butcher one head of my cattle, and I'll take your hide to the barn door and set it afire. Got that?"

"I don't make the rules, here. Del Coombs calls the turn."

"Better think twice before you turn those butcher boys loose on my stock."

Out of the corner of his eye, Brad saw Raskin leading Rose toward him. Then, an aproned man stepped outside of the cookshack. Raskin said something, and the man turned quickly and ran back inside.

"Get a move on," Brad ordered, and Raskin trotted up to him, handed him the reins.

"Toad, you drop your gunbelt, too, and kick it away from you."

Brad swung into the saddle. Rose turned in a tight circle as Toad let his gunbelt drop to the ground. He kicked it a foot away and kept his eye on it as if measuring the distance.

"Now, turn tail you two, and get to runnin'," Brad said.

The aproned man emerged from the shack with two others. All three carried rifles. But Toad and Raskin were running for all they were worth.

Brad reined up Rose and leveled his pistol at the first man who shouldered his rifle.

He cracked off a shot, aiming to a spot just above the man's head. The Colt belched sparks and white smoke, and the bullet sizzled just over the butcher's head, hit something well behind him, and whined off in tumbling flight.

Brad put the spurs to Rose's tender flank, and the horse leaped beneath him in a tight turn. He heard the crack of a rifle and heard the bullet whiz past him. Two other shots rang out before he ducked and holstered his pistol. He rode Rose hard to where Ginger was tethered. He jerked up his horse's reins and rode at a fast clip up out of the swale and onto the road.

Rose galloped on, and Ginger kept up.

A half hour later, Brad rode up a slope and hid in the trees. He waited.

None of the men followed him.

He rode north toward Oro City where he hoped to pick up some information about Delbert Coombs and find out where Felicity, Pilar, and the rest of his cattle were.

Coombs was pretty smart, but all men made mistakes. And he had already made one. He sent two stupid waddies to do a man's job, and they had been caught red-handed. Rustlers. The scum of the earth as far as Brad was concerned.

Perhaps, he thought, Julio has had better luck in finding Pilar and Felicity.

A day's ride to Oro City and he would know, one way or the other.

He settled down for the trek, his gaze ever watchful on his back trail.

But his luck still held.

And his hunger gnawed at him until he swapped horses and got into his saddlebags, dug out hardtack and jerky. He gobbled the food down as he rode on toward an uncertain destination.

TWENTY-FIVE

∾

Julio followed the tracks across dry streambeds and the gouged out ruins of old placer mines. The land was desolate, broken, filled with rubble left behind by miners when the gold ran out a few years before. There were the rotting and crumbling remains of sluice boxes and dry rockers, rusted airtights, scraps of worn leather, picks, shovels. It was as if the wind and flooding had ripped everything away and left only detritus.

He passed old graves with the wooden markers tilted and decaying, a mound with a bare rock for a headstone, the lettering in whitewash long since scrubbed away by rain and wind.

The trail was easy to follow, for a time, but gradually, as the terrain turned to rock and then to sand, he found it difficult to find the specific hoof marks of Tito, Carlos's horse. But he did find them, and after a while, when the eyestrain became too much to bear, with the sun glinting off sandstone and rock, he just followed the spoor of the driven cattle.

The tracks wound through empty, deserted canyons and

dry arroyos where lizards basked on flat stones and the buzzing of flies was the only sound he heard. Gold miners had depleted every promising stream, not only of dust, but of water and life. The land rose and fell beneath Chato's hooves. Gentle rises led to desolate vistas, and promising valleys turned to stone. Julio could not stop thinking about Pilar and wondering where she was, who the men were that held her captive. And he shuddered inwardly at what those men might do to such a pretty and delicate woman. His woman.

Finally, Julio ran out of day. The tracks became more difficult to see as the trail led through even more rugged country but always heading north toward Oro City or east only to twist back to the west.

The sun set, sinking below the far mountains with a blaze of glory, with painted ribbons and loaves of clouds, with cathedral rays that gave the sky the look of a stained glass window in a Catholic church. The night came on suddenly, and he knew he could go no farther. There were no landmarks that he could see beyond his own location, and the tracks dimmed to hieroglyphics that were like the scrawls of scorpions wriggling across sand.

He found high ground with some scrub pines that were several yards off the trail, and there he made his dry camp as the dusk swallowed everything up and the sky turned black velvet with stars strewn in every direction like scattered diamonds. He nibbled on hardtack and jerky, drank from his canteen, and lay down on his bedroll. He was tired, and Chato was worn out. He left the horse saddled and hobbled him on a sparse patch of grass. In the morning, Julio told himself, he would continue his journey to find Pilar and take her from the men who had captured her. The ground was hard under his bedroll, and the chill air crept through his blanket clear to his bones. He wished he had a serape to wear over his thin denim jacket that Pilar had patched at the sleeves with remnants of a flour sack. His toes were icy cold, and he drew himself up into a ball before he could fall asleep.

In the morning, he awoke shivering just before the dawn light split the sky with a seam of pale cream. He brushed a scorpion off his blanket, and it scuttled into the darkness with a faintly metallic whisper. He dipped grain from his saddlebag, and Chato nibbled it all away, slurping the last of it with his black tongue.

Julio could feel the chill of the earth being drawn out of the ground by the sun, and he shivered for another few minutes before he felt the first warming rays. The dew on the tracks quickly evaporated. He followed the tracks through a narrow canyon that was as bleak as any he'd ever seen, but there were no traces of mining, just talus reminders at the bases of both walls. He emerged into a barren stretch of land where only a few stunted trees grew and even sparser grass. At its far edge, the cow and horse tracks disappeared as if they had been scrubbed away. He looked closer and saw that men had whisked away the tracks for a good long stretch. So, he followed the dusted trail. Something caught his eye, and he rode off down a slope to look at it.

There was a broken sign that had tumbled down into a shallow gully. The wood was weather-beaten and had turned gray, but there was a word cut into its flat surface: Rustic.

A thought flashed through Julio's mind. He stopped and looked around him. He had never been there before, but he knew that name. He must be near the old Rustic Mine, which was almost as well known as the Lead Hill, where the miners had discovered the mother lode. Julio's pulse quickened, and he remembered the names of other mines that had brought in a bonanza for the town of Oro City: the Chrysalis, Matchless, Morning Star, Iron Silver, Little Pittsburgh, and Catalpa. All ghostly now in the aftermath of a boom that had lasted from 1859 until just a couple of years ago, when Brad had come into the country, seeking a place of solitude and serenity. Oro City was now little more than a ghost town, but there was talk that another discovery was in the wind and just about to happen. And that was something neither he nor Brad wanted.

Some said there was silver in the harsh land around Oro City, and geologists and mining engineers, along with dreamers and old prospectors, still held out hope that Oro City would spring to life again.

Julio rode down a long slope and saw an old creek running through a wide, stony bed. And there, just barely visible, he saw new lumber fashioned into pens for stock. He heard the bawling cattle a few minutes before he saw them, all straining to get out of their pens, bellowing and pushing against the poles and boards, raising a dust that hung over them like a murky cloud.

He saw men a few moments later and turned Chato away, looking for a place to stake him out so he could continue on foot.

He found such a place in a small draw, one hill away from the site of the old Rustic Mine. He tethered him to a big chunk of timber that must have been made of oak since it was hard as a rock. Like the sign, it was weathered gray, and when he picked it up, he smelled the faint odor of creosote.

He took his rifle from its sheath, filled a shirt pocket with spare cartridges, and crept up to the top of the hill and lay flat on his stomach next to a prickly pear cactus and a clump of ocotillo.

Julio looked down on what had once been the Rustic. The old ramshackle buildings were there, but new ones had been added on, some with whipsawed lumber, others constructed of logs. There were at least four stock pens and three of them were filled.

He saw a man with a maul walk up to two men wearing short leather aprons who were holding a large steer by the front and hind legs. They also had a cow flattened on the ground. The man with the maul held it over his head and then brought it down full force, smashing the steer in the forehead. The steer collapsed into a heap and didn't quiver or kick. Then one of the aproned men took out a large skinning knife and cut off the steer's right ear. He threw the ear into a big tub and wiped the blade of his knife on his canvas trousers.

Julio winced. He knew what they were doing. Two men dragged the cow toward one of the buildings. Two other men came out and dragged the dead steer inside. Laughter billowed out from the butcher shop, and the two men started chasing down another steer to kill.

There were two horses tied up at a hitch rail in front of one of the old buildings. He recognized one of the horses as belonging to Carlos. It was Tico, switching his bobbed tail and standing there with a drooping head. There was no sign of Pilar.

Then he saw two men just beyond the horses, sitting on a wooden bench. They were not butchers but hard cases. They were covered with trail dust. One of them wore two small pistols and had a protruding Adam's apple. He had a brushy mustache that he groomed with one hand while he smoked a quirley. The other man was nondescript, with a hatchet face stubbled with the iron filings of a four-day beard. He was shorter than the mustachioed man and had a hawk nose and narrow, deep-set eyes.

Julio believed those were the two men who had driven the stolen herd here.

So, he wondered, had Pilar been riding double? The thought made his blood boil. He could not picture her even riding a horse, and he knew she had never ridden double.

There was much to puzzle over as he watched the two men. He wanted to kill them. Right then and there, he wanted to put bullets into their heads or chests.

His anger was clouding his judgment, he knew. While the butchers were not armed except for knives and sledge-hammers, these two looked as if they knew how to sling lead.

Where was Pilar?

Julio looked at all the buildings. He looked at the windows, trying to see inside. From that distance, two hundred yards, at least, he saw nothing. Was Pilar tied up in one of them?

The two men got up and walked toward a pump at one end of a watering trough. The man with the two pistols threw away his stub of a rolled cigarette, and the other man worked the pump. They were closer now, almost beneath Julio, and he could see their features more clearly. And, he could hear them.

"Wish't we had that little Mex gal with us, Ridley, 'stead of just her horse."

"Old Del will take care of that little enchilada, Abner, don't you worry about it none."

"I ain't, but we might just as well go on into town and meet up with Del and Hiram. Maybe Del will pass her around."

Ridley laughed.

"They's about as much chance of that as you findin' a chunk of gold in the Rustic."

Ridley drank from the stream, then pumped water for Abner. Both men washed their faces, patted dust from their shirts.

As they walked away, he heard one of the men say, "I'll be glad to get my own horse back and get rid of that bobtail. He rides like a fence rail, sure as shit."

The voices faded away as Julio slid backward. He had heard enough.

Pilar was not at the Rustic.

She was with someone named Del, and he figured that to be one Delbert Coombs, the man who had stolen the Seguin cattle, murdered the family, burned down their house.

That same *hijo de puta*, he thought to himself. That same *hijo de mala leche*.

That same bastard. That same son of a whore.

He knew he had to find his way to Oro City. He was lost. There was nothing to do but follow those two men into town.

He wished Brad were with him, but he was already gaining a little confidence in his tracking ability.

The two hard cases would lead him to Delbert Coombs. And Pilar.

He rode with a heavy heart and he followed the tracks of the two men at a distance.

He also rode with anger, a boiling, fire-breathing monster that made him forget all about fatigue, hunger, and human kindness.

His cheekbones glowed with a red flame that was almost like war paint when the light was just right.

Julio's grandfather was a Spaniard from Barcelona. His grandmother was a full-blooded Yaqui. That was her blood reddening his high cheekbones, flaring on them like a Guanajuato sunset.

TWENTY-SIX

❦

The cabin was nestled in a grove of tall pine trees, with a wide clearing in front of it that flanked both sides of a winding lane. The place was secluded and offered a good field of view for those inside the log-frame, two-story dwelling, with its gunports in shuttered windows and at key points to the side and below each window. In back of the house were sheer craggy cliffs. There was a large log barn, a long carriage house full of empty buckboards, a separate stable for horses, a large corral, watering troughs, a deep well. In front of the lane, a creek ran by, and there was a large, flat bridge wide enough for two wagons and a four-foot-high rock wall running from both sides of the bridge to the bordering timber. It was a home, but it was also a fortress.

Delbert and Hiram, along with Pilar and Felicity, rode over the bridge and up to the house. The horses' hooves clattered on the wooden bridge, and as they approached, the snouts of a pair of rifles poked through two of the gunports flanking the front door.

"Hello, the house," Delbert called out. "It's me and Hiram."

The rifles slipped back out of sight.

The two men dismounted and tied their horses to hitch rings set just beside a flagstone path to the porch. Hiram pulled Pilar from her horse, while Delbert assisted Felicity in dismounting.

"Untie the Mex," Del ordered while he began to loosen Felicity's bonds.

"Finally," Felicity said, rubbing her wrists and dropping the twine to the ground in a frizzy tangle.

Pilar rubbed her wrists, too, and dipped a little as her swollen ankles gave way. Hiram kept her from falling.

"Follow me," Delbert said, and walked to the front door. There was no porch. He tapped three times, waited, and tapped once more. The door opened, and a white-haired lady stepped into view. Her hair was piled high, and she wore a large barrette to keep her hair in place. She had on an apron, and bound to her waist by a gunbelt gleaming with cartridges was a holster and a .44 Colt. She smiled at Delbert, flattening some of the wrinkles on her cheeks, revealing a snaggletooth and yellowed teeth.

"Why, Delbert," she said, opening her arms to give him a hug. "And you've brought guests. Two young ladies. My, my, and Hiram, dear, so good to see you both. Come in, come in. Sister's in the kitchen, stirring up a stew. Pa's upstairs, and your cousin Phil is . . . Phil"—she turned her head toward the side window—"put that rifle down and come greet your cousins."

There was a clatter and a tall, broad-shouldered young man appeared just behind Delbert's mother, Maude. Phil was a big lunk of a man in his early twenties, with straw hair and wide-set blue eyes that were pale as a blue heron feather. Wide shoulders that tapered down to a waspish waist on which hung a gunbelt and a holstered .44 Colt.

"Howdy, cuz," he said to Delbert.

Delbert ignored him and swept past his mother as she stepped aside.

"Golly, you got a couple of gals with ye," Phil Coster said, in a slow Georgian drawl.

"You never mind about that, Phil," Maude said. "You run upstairs and get your uncle Jeter. Run along."

Phil lumbered off into the gloom of the front room and soon he could be heard clambering up the stairs in his work boots.

"Ma," Delbert said, "I want you to keep these gals for me until I get back from town. Don't let 'em out of your sight."

"Sit down, Del, sit down," Maude said. "So, you got yourself a pair of hostages, eh? Any trouble?"

"Nary," Del said, motioning the two women to sit on the divan. "Their men weren't there, so they may come a-lookin', if'n you know what I mean."

"Sure do. Hiram, you sit over there in that straight-back. Pa will want his own chair when he comes down. Del, set yourself. How did you do, anyways?"

"Got the whole herd, Ma," Hiram said. "Pert near two hunnert head." He took off his hat and held it by the brim in both hands.

Del kept his hat on, and he didn't sit back in his chair but just on the edge.

"My, my," Maude said to Hiram. "Pretty darned good I'd say." Then she looked at Delbert, took a seat on another straight-back chair, and tapped back a strand of hair that had worked loose over her left ear. "So, you got deliveries to make, Del, and you look like you're about to pounce."

"I got to get into town, Ma," Delbert said. "Wagons are already rolling to Denver, Cañon City, and Pueblo. Ridley's bringing a couple of sides of beef out here to you and Pa. And, by the time I get to town, the Clarendon will be scratchin' out new menus."

Two sets of footsteps clumped down the stairs. Jeter Coombs and Phil came into the room. Jeter stood in front of Del, chewing on his pipe. He carried a heavy Henry .44 rifle with a brass receiver. He, too, wore a gunbelt and a .44 hogleg.

"I heard it, boy," he said. "You done right good. Lotta beeves, eh?"

"Enough to fill all the orders."

"I always said you was the smartest in the family, cutting prices on beef, settin' up chow houses all over creation. Pretty damned smart."

"Set down, Jeter," Maude said, and the small, gray-bearded old man with thinning hair and a rosy bulbous nose sat in the big easy chair that was covered with cowhide and stuffed with cotton and wood shavings. The chair made a wheezing sound when he sat in it and leaned his rifle against an armrest.

He didn't even look at the two women on the divan but puffed on his pipe, wreathing his head in a scarf of blue smoke.

Felicity stared at the family members, comparing their looks and their actions to Delbert's. Pilar's hand crept to hers and furtively squeezed it.

"What're you going to do in town, Del?" Phil asked.

"Collect some money for one thing," Delbert said. "Sleep. Drink some whiskey. See my gal."

"Can I go with you?"

"Hell no," Delbert said. Maude gave Phil a sharp look, and he dropped down to sit on the floor, cross-legged, his hair sticking out like an explosion of straw, a sheepish look on his face.

"What about these two doves?" Jeter said, finally looking at the two women on the divan. "They don't look like whores."

"Pa," Maude said.

"Well, his gal's a whore, ain't she?"

"You mind your manners, Jeter," she said. "These gals are Del's hostages. He wants us to look after them."

Delbert looked at Phil, then at his father.

"If they run, you either catch 'em right quick, Pa, or you shoot 'em. Got that, cousin Phil?"

"Is that what you do with hostages?" Phil asked.

"That's what you do with these two. And anybody rides up lookin' for 'em, you shoot them, too."

"Who might that be?" Jeter asked.

"Don't know what they look like. Hiram does. Hiram?"

"One's a Mex," Hiram said, "the other's a white man, kinda tall, brown hair, maybe, and he got an eagle look to him."

"What's an eagle look?" Maude asked.

"Oh, you know. He sees everything, looks everywhere all the time. Only saw him once't or twice, Ma. Big feller. Wide shoulders. A damned cowboy."

"Ho ho," Jeter said. "Just my kind of meat." He held an imaginary rifle to his shoulder and sighted down the imaginary barrel and pulled an imaginary trigger.

Everyone in the room laughed except Felicity and Pilar.

Felicity sat up straight and gave Jeter a dirty look. He reared back, surprised.

"You're all a heartless pack of . . . wolves," she said. "My husband will be coming after me, and Pilar's husband, too. They're both good shots."

"Well, now," Jeter said, "we'll give 'em both a kindly welcome, little lady. Don't you worry your pretty head about that."

"Your sons stole our cattle and burned down our houses and our barn," she said. "How can you live with yourselves?"

"You mind your tongue, missy," Maude cut in. "Don't go castin' no stones."

"They's some what grows cows," Jeter said, taking his corncob pipe from his mouth, "and others what takes 'em to market. Who in hell do you think is smarter?"

"It's still stealing," Felicity said. "You're all criminals."

"Now, don't you be callin' the kettle black, missy," Maude said. "You ain't without sin. Ain't nobody is."

Felicity just glared at Maude, too furious to speak.

Pilar squeezed her hand as if to warn her.

Del got up.

"Hiram's going to be riding guard tonight," he said.

"He knows what them two jaspers look like. You hear him shoot, you get ready."

"You mind your tracks comin' in here, Del?" Jeter asked.

"I don't expect they'll find us out here, at least not right away. We covered our tracks pretty well."

He walked over to the divan and looked down at Felicity.

"I got a permanent room at the Clarendon, Felicity," he said. "I'll come back for you in a day or two. You might like livin' high on the hog."

She could not escape the look of lust on Delbert's face. He was undressing her with that look, and she could feel his rough hands on her breasts. She wanted to cringe, but she wasn't going to give him the satisfaction.

"Delbert," she said, "go sleep with your whore. You'd have to kill me before I'd give you the time of day."

"Bitch," he said, suddenly angry. He brought himself under control then and touched a finger to the brim of his hat. "I like bitches. If they claw and scream, I like 'em even better. Be seein' you, Felicity."

She wanted to spit at him as he turned to go, but she just sat there and fumed silently.

Then she saw the look in Hiram's eyes and in Phil's, and sank back on the divan, trying to make herself as small as possible.

Pilar sighed and crossed herself quickly. She looked heavenward, a deep confusion in her mind.

She felt as if they had been brought to an insane asylum, and she was afraid. She was dirty and sweaty and very tired. Her body ached from sleeping on hard ground, and her buttocks were tender from riding. She missed Julio and prayed that he could come soon and deliver her from these godless and cruel people.

Delbert closed the door behind him, and the room was silent for a moment.

Maude looked at Pilar and Felicity. She smiled a wan smile.

"I've got just the room for you two," she said. "It ain't got no winders, and it's pretty cramped. But it has two cots in it, and I can lock it up tight at night."

Felicity glared at her.

"If'n you misbehave, I just might give the key to Hiram or Phil after we turn down the lamps."

Felicity stared at the woman in disbelief. Maude had that same look on her face that she had seen on Delbert's.

Felicity knew that she had somehow finally met a group of people who were more than criminals.

They were pure evil.

The most evil people she had ever encountered.

And Brad could not find her soon enough.

TWENTY-SEVEN

❧

Brad was astonished to see the old town of Oro City teeming with people. He knew that they had incorporated the town early in 1878 after a couple of geologists discovered carbonite, and there was talk of mining lead. Lead mining might bring the town back to life, the old-timers said. Oro City had died when the gold ran out, but now the population had swelled with men digging out lead instead of gold.

He rode to the High Grade and saw that it was no longer a ramshackle saloon hanging onto the past but had a new false front and sign, and a much bigger floor space, complete with glitter gals in their skimpy lace, brocade skirts, and bodices. He tied Ginger to an empty hitch rail and walked through newly varnished batwing doors. A tinkling piano sounded from the far corner and nearly every table was filled. He couldn't see much until his eyes adjusted to the shift of light, but then he saw empty spaces at the long bar, which, he noticed, was also new.

He found an empty stool at the far end of the bar and sat down. He felt out of place in the din, and none of the girls paid him any mind so busy were they plying the tables, flirting with hard-rock miners, young dandies, and fat men in business suits puffing on cigars.

A barkeep wearing a red brocade vest and black armbands, with a small apron tied around his waist, walked up to Brad.

"What's your pleasure, Mister," the bartender said.

"Beer cold?"

"It ain't frozen, but it's fairly cool."

"Pull me a draft of the coolest, then."

"That trail dust on you, or you been diggin' on Carbonite Hill?"

Brad laughed.

"Does it show that much?"

"Mister, you look like a cowman who's been ridin' drag for forty mile."

Brad laughed again.

"Well, I'm no lead miner."

"There's more than lead being mined."

"I thought the gold ran out."

"It sure did. But they been findin' veins of silver in that carbonite. It's a regular bonanza all over again. You still need a hot bath."

"I'll wash up at the Excelsior," he said. "Just got into town."

"How long's it been since you've been here? The Excelsior burned down about a year or so ago, when we was old Oro City."

"Been that long, I guess. So, the hotel didn't rebuild?"

"Nope."

"What's the best hotel in town, then?"

"That'd be the Clarendon. Might be full up."

"I'll look around."

"Try Main Street or State Street. You might find somethin'."

"Thanks," Brad said.

The bartender brought him a glass mug filled with beer and two inches of foam. The beer was tepid but washed the dust out of his throat. He learned the barkeep's name was Larry. Larry didn't ask him his, and looking around, Brad could see why. Men came and went, dozens of them, most looking down-and-out. Brad didn't see Julio anywhere, but he saw several Mexicans sitting at tables, smoking cigarettes, and eyeing the young women.

Brad sipped his beer and felt lightheaded after a few swallows. He didn't want to get drunk, but he was so hungry he could eat the south end of a northbound horse. He kept looking at the batwings, hoping to see Julio come in. It had been three days, and this was where he had told Julio to meet him.

Larry walked by every so often and looked at Brad's glass. When it was nearly empty, Larry leaned over the bar.

"Ready for another?"

"In a minute. You ever hear tell of a man named Delbert Coombs. He's got a brother named Hiram."

Larry's expression changed.

The ready smile was gone, the laughter in his eyes had faded. Instead, the corners of his mouth bent downward and his eyebrows raised a good quarter inch and his eyes narrowed slightly.

"You got business with the Coombs boys?"

"Maybe."

"I took you for a cattleman or sheepherder, Mister, not one of that bunch."

"I'm not looking for a job with Coombs."

"Good. Delbert and his whole bunch have a bad reputation in certain parts of town."

"I never met the man," Brad said.

"Then, why do you ask about him?"

"Maybe you can tell me something about that reputation he has in certain parts."

"I could, but I ain't goin' to. Del Coombs carries a lot of weight in Oro City.

"That could mean anything."

"Let's say he's on the shady side of the law. Nobody can prove anything, but he's big in the beef business. Supplies all the hotels and eating establishments from here clear to Denver and points in between with fresh beef."

"Where does he get his beef?" Brad asked.

Larry shrugged and looked around him to see if anyone was in earshot. They were alone.

"Nobody knows. But some people ask. Them who ask too loud don't come in the High Grade no more."

"What do you mean, Larry? Exactly."

"I mean you don't see those folks no more. Like sheriffs and lawmen who come here and start askin' questions. You ain't packin' a star under that shirt, are you?"

Larry looked at the slight bulge in Brad's shirt. The rattles.

Brad shook his head.

"I'm no lawman," he said.

"What's your business with Coombs, if I might ask?"

"It's about some beef missing from my ranch, Larry, but I don't want that information bandied about."

"You sayin' Del Coombs rustled your beef?"

"About two hundred head."

Larry let out a low whistle and scratched his head.

"Something wrong?" Brad asked.

"I've been here since the gold rush," he said. "Seen 'em come and go. Seen ranchers who used to come to town, come in here to wet their thirst. Heard 'em talk about drivin' cattle to Denver or sellin' their beeves in Pueblo. First thing you know, they don't come here no more and Del's selling meat. Not on the hoof but already dead and ready to be cut into steaks and chops, turned into filets, T-bones, sirloins, and ground up for the Mexes."

"And no more ranchers," Brad said.

"No proof of rustling, neither. No sir, you're the first man I seen in here who got rustled and lived to tell about it."

"You've been a big help, Larry. I'll take another of those draft beers."

"Coombs has him a permanent room at the Clarendon. More like a fancy suite."

"Thanks."

Larry stood up.

"If you go up against him, you don't stand a chance, Mister. Any one of his cronies would rub you out without battin' an eye."

"What makes you think I wouldn't do the same to them?"

"I didn't think you were a crazy man. I could be wrong, though."

Larry walked away, taking Brad's empty glass. He held it under the spigot of a tapped keg and filled it slowly. He took a wooden spoon that was almost flat and wiped away the top of the foam and poured a small amount of beer in the glass.

"Four bits," he said, setting the glass in front of Brad. "Forgot to charge you for the first one."

"Two bits for a beer? Price has gone up," Brad said.

"Like I said, Oro City is a boom town." He smiled as Brad laid out a pair of quarters. They clattered on the bartop. Larry scooped them up.

"Case you're wonderin'," he said, "none of the Coombs boys are here today. Been gone the better part of a month. But I hear the Clarendon got in a shipment of beef last night. Fresh beef."

He walked away, and Brad stared after him. What was he getting into? How many men did Delbert Coombs have? At least six, he figured, from reading the tracks. Six against one. Or six against two if Julio showed up.

But he might not have to face them all at once. He had only seen two of them. Which meant two of them had seen him. If he saw those two, he would recognize them. And, they would recognize him.

He did not know what Delbert or his brother, Hiram, looked like. But they were the honchos, evidently.

Should he go to the local sheriff and file a complaint against Coombs? Did he have proof that they rustled his cattle? Not with him, but maybe that stockyard where he had braced Toad and Freddie might have enough evidence of rustled beef to offer a court of law. Did they even have a court of law in Oro City?

Brad did not know.

So many questions, he thought. He knew where Coombs stayed now, but how far could he go without the law on his side? And what if the law was on Delbert's payroll? There was something very rotten about a town that harbored such a man, a killer and a rustler who had been getting away with his crimes for years.

The batwing doors swung open, and Brad saw the silhouette of a man enter the saloon. He could not see anything but an outline, but the figure looked familiar.

The man stepped inside and turned his head, looking around the room. Brad raised his hand.

Julio saw Brad and began walking toward him, slow at first, then faster and faster the closer he got.

Brad motioned to the empty stool next to him.

"Sit down," he said, in Spanish.

Julio beamed.

"I am glad to see you, Brad," he said. "Did you find Felicity?"

"No. What about Pilar?"

"They tricked us, those men. Pilar was not with the ones I tracked. They changed the horses to fool us."

"They sure did. Will you take a drink?"

Julio looked at the beer in front of Brad.

"Maybe I will drink *una cerveza*," he said. "*Tengo mucho hambre*."

"Yeah, I'm hungry, too."

Brad waited for Larry to turn around, then beckoned to him and pointed to his glass and held up one finger.

"Tell me all you know, Julio," he said.

"Only if you tell me what you have found out, *mi jefe*."

"You might have to drink two beers before we eat, Julio."

"I do not care. I also have hunger for knowledge, knowledge about my Pilar and your Felicity."

"Well, I found Rose. She is in the stable getting shod. So we have a horse for Carlos. And, we may need him."

"You know something, then."

"I know something."

Larry brought the beer, and Brad paid him two bits.

"It's good you have a friend here, Mister," the barkeep said. "You might need a few more."

Julio looked puzzled.

"What does he say?"

"I'll tell you everything I know, Julio. Just tell me what you saw, what you learned."

Julio put the glass to his lips, drank through the foam. His lips were lathered, and he wiped them with his sleeve.

"I saw two men," he said. "One was riding Tico. I mean he was not riding him, but Tico was there. They were two of the rustlers."

"Do you know their names?"

"One was called Ridley, I think. I think the other was called Abner. I do not know which one was riding Tico. But Tico is tied up outside this cantina. I did not see the other horse outside."

"What? Do you mean one of the men is here? Right in here?"

"I do not know. I only saw you, *patrón*."

"Well, look around, Julio. Take your time. Tell me if you see either of the men you tracked."

Julio craned his neck. He looked around the room, then along the bar.

He ducked his head as if trying to hide behind his glass of beer.

"He is here, at the other end of the bar. The man standing next to a pretty girl. He is one of those I saw."

"You sure?"

"Yes, I am sure. I do not know if that is the Ridley one. I—I do not remember."

"It doesn't make any difference. Thanks."

"What will you do, Brad?"

Brad could not answer Julio's question just then. He was studying the man, memorizing his features.

The man had his arm around one of the glitter gals. He seemed to know her. They were both smiling. Laughing. And drinking.

So, he thought, the High Grade is the gang's watering hole. And one of the chickens had come home to roost. That was a good sign. It reminded him of hunting pronghorn antelope on the plains. He just waited for them to come to the watering hole. He picked out the one he wanted, took aim, and pulled the trigger. He and Felicity ate antelope that night.

"Well," he said to Julio, his voice pitched low, "we found their watering hole. Ever hunt antelope, Julio?"

TWENTY-EIGHT

～

Brad saw the puzzlement on Julio's face. But he had already made up his mind, and there was no time to explain. He beckoned to Larry, who was heading their way, his hands holding five or six glasses by their rims. Larry dropped the empty glasses in a tub of wash water behind the bar and came up to the end where Brad and Julio were sitting.

"Two questions, Larry, if you wouldn't mind?"

"I can handle two, maybe."

"The name of that jasper at the other end of the bar with his hand inside that lady's blouse."

Larry turned his head and looked.

"That's Wicks. Abner Wicks. He's one of Delbert's men."

"Where's the sheriff's office these days?"

"Middle of State Street."

"His name?"

"That's one question over the limit, friend." There was a sardonic smile on Larry's face.

"I owe you, Larry."

"Our new sheriff, still slightly wet behind the ears, is Rodney Dimsdale."

"Thanks," Brad said, standing up. He looked at Julio. "Let's go, Julio. We're going to get Tico back for Carlos."

Julio slid from his stool.

"You didn't finish your beers, gents," Larry said. "And, say, I didn't get your name, Mister."

"I didn't give it, Larry. But you can call me Sidewinder for now."

"Sidewinder? That your real name?"

Brad didn't answer. He and Julio were already walking briskly down to the other end of the bar.

"What we do, Brad?" Julio whispered.

"Just back me up, Julio. We're going to do a little horse trading."

"You give me the confusion sometimes, Brad."

"I confuse myself sometimes, Julio."

Brad stepped close to the man named Abner Wicks.

"Sir," he said, "may I have a word with you?"

Wicks turned around, saw the two men standing there, one of them a Mexican. He had the feeling he should know them.

"What's on your mind, stranger?"

"I wondered if you wanted to sell that bobtailed dun with the cropped mane you have hitched outside."

"Huh?"

"I'm buying," Brad said.

"I ain't sellin'," Wicks said.

"Well, I'm taking the horse, Wicks," Brad said.

Abner's hand shot off the girl's shoulder and dropped to the butt of his pistol.

"You what?" Abner said, his tone sharp as a razor's honed edge.

"You heard me, Wicks."

"How'd you know my name?"

"Why, I picked it out of the pig slop, Wicks."

"Them's fightin' words, Mister."

"You pull that hogleg, Wicks, and I'll drop you where you stand. There's two of us and just one of you."

Brad kept his voice low so that only Julio, the glitter gal, and Wicks could hear him. But Abner saw Brad's hand hovering over the butt of his pistol like a hawk about to fold its wings and dive.

"You put it that way . . ." he said.

"Let's just step outside and take a look at that bobtailed dun, Wicks. Lady, you better light a shuck to other parts."

The woman scurried away, white-faced, her skirt rustling like wind through a cornfield.

"Step away from the bar and go through those batwings, Wicks. We'll be right behind you."

"You got a lot of cheek, Mister," Wicks said.

But he went out the swinging doors and walked to where Tico stood hipshot.

"Take a look at that brand, Wicks," Brad said. He pointed to the horse's right rump. "That's the Box B from the Baron ranch in Texas. I bought that horse from Anson Baron himself. I've got the papers."

"I don't know nothin' about that," Wicks said.

"Well, let me put it this way, Wicks. That makes you a horse thief. And that's a hanging offense."

Wicks blanched.

"Take Tico, Julio, and follow me and Mr. Wicks."

"Where we goin'?" Wicks asked.

Brad stepped forward and lifted the pistol from Abner's holster and held it leveled at Abner's gut.

"We're going to pay a call on Sheriff Dimsdale," Brad said. "Now, step out."

"Bastard," Wicks muttered, but started marching toward State Street. Julio followed, leading Tico.

The sheriff was in.

He looked up from his desk when Brad ushered Wicks through the door.

The man sitting behind the desk wore a star on his chest. There were three other men in the room: a young deputy, who also wore a badge; a man in a business suit with a hand-painted tie dangling from his collar; and an-

other man, younger, who was dressed like a banker, minus
the coat. They all stared intently at Brad and Wicks.

"What do we have here?" Dimsdale said. He was a
balding, forty-year-old man with carious teeth and a pock-
marked face that looked weathered from more than wind
but was likely from a steady diet of corn whiskey. He wore
red suspenders and a striped shirt, baggy pants with food
stains embedded in the light fabric. He had a small button
of a nose that looked like a mashed mushroom.

"You know Abner Wicks here, Sheriff?" Brad said.

"Don't know him well. Know who he is. That his pistol
in your hand?"

"It is."

"Well, now, I'll just have that, and your name and some
quick explanation," Dimsdale said.

Brad handed him the Colt, butt first. Dimsdale took it,
opened a drawer, and stuck the gun inside.

"My name's Bradley Storm, and this man stole my horse,
that bobtailed dun out there with the Mexican."

"Got proof?"

"No. Just my word. I also want to charge him with cattle rustling and destruction of property. My property. My
cattle."

"No proof, you say." Dimsdale looked over at the man
in the business suit. He had long sideburns salted with gray
hairs, a neatly trimmed mustache, and small goatee. He
wore a vest with a watch chain dangling from one pocket.
His coat was open and the lining appeared to be made of
painted silk. He returned Dimsdale's look with a nod.

"This feller and others, including two brothers named
Coombs, not only stole two hundred head of cattle, but
burned down my house, two bunkhouses, and my barn. So,
I have no proof of anything. They picked me clean and
burned all my proof."

"What's your name again?" Dimsdale asked.

"Storm. Brad Storm."

"Well, Mr. Storm, I might be able to help you. Might, I

said, just might." He looked over at the young man who was wearing a smaller star than his and spoke to him. "Wally, you take Wicks here and put him in cell one."

"We only got one cell," Wally said, rising from his rickety chair.

"Then, that's the one."

Wally Culver grabbed Wicks's arm and led him across the room to a closed door. He opened the door and the two disappeared after he closed it behind him. Brad heard the jingling of keys and the slam of an iron door.

"You'll charge Wicks with horse thieving, cattle rustling, arson, and kidnapping?" Brad asked.

"Who'd he kidnap?" Dimsdale asked.

"My wife and the wife of that man outside with the dun horse."

Again Dimsdale looked over at the man in the business suit.

"Well, now, not so fast, Mr. Storm. First, I want you to meet a man who might be interested in hearing your story."

The man in the business suit got up from his chair, walked over to stand next to Brad. The man looked Brad up and down with keen gray eyes. He stroked his goatee a couple of times.

"Storm, this is Mr. Harry Pendergast. He's head of the Denver Detective Agency. Just rode into town."

Pendergast held out his hand. Brad shook it.

"Nice to meet you, Mr. Storm. I'd like you to meet one of my agents. Pete, come over here."

The other man got up and shook Brad's hand. "This is Pete Farnsworth. He's been staying here in Oro . . . I mean Oro City, for the past several months. I'd like to buy you a meal or a drink and discuss your case with you, sir."

Brad looked at the sheriff.

"He can do more for you than I can, Storm," Dimsdale said. "I'll hold Wicks as long as I can."

"Come with us, Mr. Storm," Pendergast said. "And bring your friend out there with us if you like."

Before he could unravel all his thoughts, Brad found himself walking outside with Pendergast and Farnsworth.

"We'll go to the Clarendon," Pendergast said. "I'm staying there while I'm in town. I have a proposition for you, Mr. Storm. And who is this?"

"Mr. Pendergast, this is Julio Aragon, my friend and a hand on my ranch. Julio, this is Harry Pendergast and Pete Farnsworth."

The men shook hands.

"Tie up Tico and come with us, Julio. Mr. Pendergast is going to buy us lunch."

"You look like you both could stand a meal, Mr. Storm," Pendergast said. "And I hope you've got some useful information for me and Pete."

"Useful, maybe. But, will you use it?"

"If it concerns Delbert Coombs and his brother, Hiram, I'll not only use it, I'll pay good money for it. That suit you, Mr. Storm?"

They walked the short distance to the Clarendon Hotel.

But not once did Pendergast bring up the name of Delbert Coombs, rustling, arson, or kidnapping. Instead, he talked about how Denver was growing and the salubrious climate of the Rocky Mountains.

Brad wondered if he'd acquired a pig in the poke without paying out a cent. Behind him, he heard Pete and Julio conversing in Spanish. But Pete wasn't touching on any recent incidents concerning them either. They were talking about the Catholic Church, the Alamo, General Santa Anna, Maximilian, and the Mexican Revolution.

They entered the hotel and walked straight to the dining room. Pendergast was met by the headwaiter, who knew him, and they were ushered to a private corner where they sat down amid potted palms and live prickly pear cactus growing in clay vessels.

"I'll order for all of us," Pendergast said, then turned to Brad.

"Mr. Storm," he said, "do you have any feelings about justice, regardless of the law?"

Brad was taken aback by the question.

He noted the smile on Pendergast's face, but it was a meaningless smile without warmth, without commitment.

The smile looked as if it had been painted there by some diabolical prankster and then shellacked over to last a thousand maddening years.

TWENTY-NINE

⌘

Pete Farnsworth, Julio Aragon, and Harry Pendergast all looked straight at Brad, waiting for his answer to Pendergast's question.

Brad felt the scrutiny and pondered his answer. He wondered if it was a trick question. But, no, it was straight enough. Just unusual. He decided that Pendergast asked it to test him, his morals, his judgment, and perhaps, his intelligence.

He looked at Julio, whose eyes brightened.

"The Mexicans have a saying," Brad said, "that I first heard from my friend, Julio. And Julio is a very wise man. The Mexicans say, '*No hay justicía en el mundo.*' In other words, there's no such thing as justice in this world.

"But, there is revenge and retribution. People say they want justice, but most of the time they just want blood."

"And what about the law, Mr. Storm?" Pendergast said.

"Which one? The written law? Those laws are for the judges, juries, and lawyers. Where there is no law or when the law fails, a man must make his own law. If he truly wants justice, he might go to the law first. If he does not get justice, then he must make a decision."

There was a momentary silence.

Brad's eyes bore right into Pendergast's.

"And, the decision?" Pendergast said.

"A man might have to take the law into his own hands, Mr. Pendergast. If there is no justice in the world, then that's a downright shame. If the law does not hand out justice and justice is cried for by a righteous man, then that man must seek justice."

"Any way he can?"

"Any way he can."

"Then there is justice in the world," Pendergast said.

"It's a question of interpretation, even with the law. Is justice the same for a rich man as it is for a poor man? Is justice the same for a landowner as it is for a share-cropper?"

"Umm, Mr. Storm, I think not," Pendergast said.

"Now, you tell me, sir, why would you ask me such a question? Surely you know that I'm not a lawman or a judge, and I've never sat on a jury. You got something in your craw, and that question tells me you've been chewing on it for quite some time."

Again, a breathless pause that lasted but a few seconds.

Pete Farnsworth cleared his throat. Pendergast picked up a napkin and tucked it into his collar like a bib.

"I think Julio and I will wash up, Mr. Pendergast," Brad said, scooting back in his chair. "Come on, Julio. Let's find the washroom."

"In the lobby," Pendergast said. "Just look for a sign that says Gents."

"Much obliged," Brad said. He and Julio walked across the dining room and into the hotel lobby.

"What do you think, Pete?" Pendergast said.

"I think you've found your man, Harry. Del Coombs is one smart man. He gave me the slip. I completely missed this one."

"How can you not have known, Pete? Honestly."

"Del's slicker than an electric eel. He has eyes in the back of his head. He's a magician. Hell, I don't know. He and his bunch left town and hit Storm without anybody even knowing they were gone."

"So, what do we do with Storm? How can we use him?"

"Let's hear what he has to say about the rustling. What puzzles me is not only why he's still alive, but how he caught Abner Wicks red-handed with that stolen horse."

"Yes, that was impressive, I must say." Pendergast twisted the tip of his goatee, then fluffed it back into its regular shape. "That's one out of the way for now."

"Five to go."

The waiter was serving the meal when Brad and Julio returned, their faces no longer dusty, but clean except for beard stubble, their hands no longer dark and grimy or clotted with sweat and sand. They sat down.

"*Bistec*," Julio said, looking at his plate.

"Those are top sirloins, gentlemen," Pendergast said, "and might be from your own herd."

Brad hesitated just a minute before cutting his steak with a knife, holding the meat down with his fork. There were boiled potatoes, pinto beans, halved pears in small bowls, and sautéed mushrooms.

"Probably not poisonous, then," Brad said. Everyone at the table laughed.

He chewed the first piece and smacked his lips.

"Yep," he said, "finest beef in the territory."

"You have a remarkable sense of humor, Mr. Storm," Pendergast said.

"Call me Brad, will you, Mr. Pendergast? I keep looking around for my father every time you call me mister."

"Then call me Harry." Pendergast flashed a wide smile and brought a glass of water to his lips.

"All right, Harry. You're a detective from Denver. You don't give a damn about a horse thief like Wicks. So, what brings you to Oro City?"

"Oh, but I do care about Wicks, Brad. In fact, I'm glad to have him locked up, even if he's in the custody of Sheriff Dimwit."

"I thought his name was Dimsdale."

Pete laughed.

"He's Dimwit to us," he said. "Scared to death of the Coombs brothers, like everybody else in town, and about as brave as a bunny rabbit."

"I'd hate to see Wicks get away from him," Brad said.

"Count on it," Pete said. "He'll set bail for Wicks, and Wicks will get out. After that, Brad, you're a marked man. Those boys will hunt you down and shoot you deader'n last month's *Denver Post*. Coombs doesn't let witnesses live very long. In fact, in his eyes, you're already an old man sitting on his deathbed."

"I know," Brad said.

"You do?" Pendergast said. "How in the devil did you manage to stay alive and yet . . . ?"

Brad interrupted him. He told him how he and Julio had been gone, hunting, he said, and what they found when they got back. He told him about tracking his herd, the switching of horses, and how he'd gotten Wicks.

"I'm impressed," Pendergast said. "But how do you know about the Coombs boys, leaving no witnesses."

"I figure these men, these criminals, have done this before. One day Julio and I were chasing after some strays and came upon the burned remains of the Seguin house. Julio told me the story."

"So you know about Alberto Seguin, do you?"

"A little. Why?"

"Do you know who was killed when he rustled Alberto's cattle?"

"Why, his wife and kids, I reckon."

"And there was a white boy who stayed with them," Julio said.

"Do you know the boy's name, Julio?" Pendergast asked.

"No. I never hear it."

"There was a boy staying with Alberto and his wife that spring and summer," Pendergast said. "He was fourteen years old, had curly brown hair, a winning smile. He was eager to learn about cattle ranching. That boy had big dreams. He was from Denver. His bones are buried in a cemetery there alongside his mother, who died of grief shortly after that boy was murdered."

"You seem to know a lot about him, Harry," Brad said. He bit into a piece of pear he had spooned out of his bowl.

Pete cleared his throat again. Pendergast's face turned the color of a Wyoming sunset. He dabbed at his mouth with the corner of his napkin. There were tears in his eyes.

"That boy was my son, Brad. His name was Randolph. We called him Randy. He was my only son, and I've been trying to bring his murderers to justice for some years now. That's why Pete is down here. It took me some time to put Delbert Coombs's operation together. In fact, that's why I formed the Denver Detective Agency. I wanted some law, some legal backing, to go after Coombs and his bunch."

Brad and Julio stopped eating. They both stared at Pendergast. Both saw the tears welling up in his eyes.

"I—I don't know what to say, Harry. I'm sorry."

"That's why you and Julio must get your wives back right away, Brad. He didn't get you and Julio or your other hand, Carlos, but he got your wives and he's using them for bait. He wants you to come after him. He wants you to find out where they are so he can kill you and them. No more witnesses. He'll kill Carlos, too. Given time. You can bet on it."

"I know that, Harry," Brad said. "Julio and I just got into town. I found out that Delbert Coombs keeps a permanent room in this very hotel."

"He does," Pete said. "He hasn't returned in two or three weeks, however. I got to know his gal, Kathy Burriss. When she shows up, I'll know Del's back here. So far, she's still staying at home with her mother."

"Pete has been working undercover for me," Pendergast said, "for six months or so. He deals monte at the

High Grade five nights a week. That's how he keeps an eye on these criminals. But, as you may know, we had no evidence until you showed up."

"I have evidence?" Brad said.

"Well, you're a witness more or less. Good enough for a Denver court, probably."

"You're going to arrest them?"

Pendergast finished his meal, pushed his chair back, reached in his pocket, and brought out four fancy cigars. He passed them around. Pete and Julio each took one. Brad shook his head.

"Trials sometimes take quite a long time, Brad," Pendergast said, "and criminals hire expensive lawyers with all the scruples of an alley cat, and, well, justice is not often served."

"What are you saying, Harry?"

Harry lit his cigar from a match he struck on the underside of his chair. He passed the lucifer to Julio, who passed it to Pete. Smoke billowed over the table, and Harry raised his hand.

The waiter came over.

"Bring us some Napoleon, Fritz," he said to the waiter, "and four snifters."

"Yes, sir, Mr. Pendergast, and I'll have this table cleared right away."

Harry did not speak again until after the table was cleared and the brandies were in snifters, the bottle still on the table. He sent a plume of smoke into the air and fixed Brad with a steady stare. His tears were gone, and he seemed very composed.

"I told you, Brad," Pendergast said, "that I had a proposition for you. Well, here it is. I want to hire you as an agent. You no longer have a ranch. You've lost all your cattle, and you'll never get them back. So, I want to hire you to work for me. Not just on this case, but as a full-time detective. I pay well, and there's plenty of work. Good, clean work. Sometimes a tad dangerous, but from what I've seen, you can handle a little danger. You and Julio here have shown me that you are good detectives. You tracked your herd, you uncovered what had been hidden for years. You know the names of the culprits, and, as far as being legal, you have enough evidence to convict. We can now send a U.S. marshal down here to visit all the old mines being used as butcher shops. They can collect evidence and convict a large group of active criminals."

"Are you offering Julio a job, too, then?"

"Absolutely. But only if you accept, of course."

"If the U.S. marshals can round them all up, then why . . ."

"Justice moves slow in these parts, Brad. Yours and Julio's wives are in immediate danger. Once word gets out that you braced Wicks and had him arrested . . ."

"How soon will that be? I mean, before Coombs finds out about Wicks?"

"Wicks will be out of jail before sunset. Nothing we can do about it. Coombs will waste no time. He'll come hunting you. Now, Pete knows where he stays, sometimes. At his folks' place, north of town, in the next range of foothills. He can take you there. That's probably where he took your women.

"His folks are as rotten as he is, and he's got a cousin that lives with him who has the brains of a pissant but is dangerous as a rattlesnake. That house is a regular fortress."

"You sure throw a lot at a man all at once, Harry," Brad said.

"I have contracts in my room upstairs, Brad. You sign them and anything you do to these men will have the full backing of the agency."

"You mean . . . ?"

"I mean, Brad, if they resist capture, you have my authorization to defend yourself in pursuit of legal reparation for a heinous crime."

"You mean you want me to kill Delbert and Hiram Coombs. Is that right?"

"Just sign the contracts, Brad. Then you can do whatever you want to."

"I want it plain, Harry. Straight and simple. This contract means what?"

"They murdered my son, Randy, Brad."

"Tell me what I can do, Harry. Tell me what you want me to do. Straight and plain."

"I want those men dead. Every one of them. And, unless I miss my guess, so do you."

"That's plain enough. I'll give them every chance to surrender, though."

"I'm sure you will, Brad," Pendergast said.

And then he smiled the widest smile Brad had ever seen.

Pendergast raised his glass and offered it as a toast. All four men clinked snifters and drank.

Harry Pendergast kept smiling while the fumes filled Brad's nose and the brandy burned all the way down to his stomach.

He felt good for the first time in many days.

Real good.

THIRTY

∽

Delbert Coombs felt his anger rising as he listened to Tod Sutphen's report. He hated incompetence, and he hated loose ends. He had built his illicit business by being competent and leaving no witnesses. Now he was seeing his latest scheme unravel like a spool of thread in a whirlwind.

"He calls himself Sidewinder, boss," Sutphen said. "But, I know it's that Storm feller. We seen him at the ranch. Him and that other Mex."

"I've already sent Ridley to see that sniveling justice of the peace, Stoval, to bail Abner out of jail. So, I know those two men are here in town. Kathy Burriss just left here with the money to give to Ridley."

Fred Raskin stood there, with his hat in his hands, admiring the hotel room. He was all agog at the plush furnishings.

"Why didn't you kill Storm, Freddie, when you had the chance?" Delbert asked. "There was two of you and one of him."

"He had the drop on us, Del, and that rattle he had spooked us pretty good."

"A trick, a damned trick, and you both fell for it."

"Man caught us by surprise," Sutphen said.

"Toad, everything catches you by surprise. Now I've got to get back to Ma's and see to it that those two women are still cards in my deck. You boys better get out there, too. Ridley will meet us all there."

"You think Storm will come after them wimmin?" Sutphen said.

"What do you think, Toad? Storm tracked Abner here, evidently, and he'll figure it out. Man's too damned smart for his chaps, you ask me."

"Yes, sir," Sutphen said.

"Now, both of you get the hell out of here. Light a shuck to Ma's and do what she tells you. Tell her I'll be along soon."

"What're you gonna do, Del?" Raskin asked.

"Take a bath," Delbert said, and ushered the men to the door.

His anger was in full bloom now, and he needed time to think. He had weeks of dirt on him, and until he got rid of Storm and that Mexican, he had to forgo the luxury of the Clarendon.

But if he was going to die, he was going to die clean.

THIRTY-ONE

Brad converted his gold dust into cash at the assessor's office while Julio and Pete waited outside. Then he paid the blacksmith for shoeing Rose. He put Rose and Tico up in the Oro City Stables, which had not yet changed its name. But a sign painter was already cleaning the sign and was ready to paint Oro City Livery on the false front.

Pete's horse was in the stables. He saddled up the rangy black gelding and met Brad and Julio outside.

"Where to now?" Brad asked.

"Out to the Coombs place. I warn you now, Brad, it's not going to be easy. That whole family is a bunch of gun slicks and no telling how many of Delbert's men are waiting there just to tack your hide up on the wall."

They rode past the Clarendon Hotel just as Sutphen and Raskin were walking out to get on their horses. Sutphen looked up when he was just stepping off the boardwalk.

There, not twenty feet away, was Storm, and both men saw each other at the same time.

"There's Toad," Brad said. "And Freddie."

"I recognize them," Pete said. "They work for Delbert Coombs."

"Hey Sidewinder," Toad called. "You done shook your last rattle."

He went for his pistol.

Brad was a split second faster. He spurred Ginger into a leap, drew his pistol, cocked the hammer as it came out of its holster, drew a bead on Sutphen, and squeezed the trigger.

Toad's pistol was clear of its holster when the .44 slug hit him square in the chest. A crimson flower bloomed over his heart, and he twisted sideways from the powerful impact. His gun fell from his limp-fingered hand and he fell to his knees, a hole in his back the size of a fist.

Raskin stepped off the boardwalk and drew his pistol.

Brad reined Ginger into a tight turn, but he didn't have a clear shot.

Pete and Julio drew their pistols, but Raskin ducked behind his horse and neither man had a clear shot.

Brad dismounted and, crouching, started toward Raskin.

Raskin hugged his horse for concealment, keeping an eye on Pete and Julio, who were scrambling their horses for a clear shot.

Brad pulled out his rattle and shook it.

Raskin jumped back in alarm.

Brad stepped onto the boardwalk and shook the rattle again.

Raskin whirled and jumped another foot away from his horse.

Out into the open.

"Drop it, Freddie," Brad said.

"Go to hell," Freddie said.

Those were the last words out of his mouth.

Brad pulled the trigger and shot Raskin just above his belt buckle. Blood spurted from the wound, and Raskin crumpled to the ground, clutching a shiny coil of intestine oozing like a snake from his stomach.

Brad stepped up to him and shook the rattle in his face.

"You can never be sure about a sidewinder," he said to Freddie. "One can come at you from any direction. Still want me to go to hell?"

"For God's sake, man, help me." Raskin squirmed in pain.

"You can die slow or die fast. Make up your mind."

"You bastard," Raskin breathed.

Julio rode in and pointed his pistol at Raskin's head. He cocked it and squeezed the trigger. The bullet smacked into Raskin's temple and blew a cupful of brains out the other side, spattering Brad with a foamy spray of blood.

"That is for stealing my wife," Julio said in English.

"He can't hear you, Julio," Brad said.

Pete let out a low whistle, then holstered his pistol.

"We'd better clear out, Brad, or get set to answer a whole bushel of questions."

Brad holstered his .44 and swung into the saddle.

"Lead on, Pete," he said.

A crowd was gathering around the two dead men. A gabble of voices rose up, and men pointed fingers down the street.

The horses kicked up dust as the three men rode to the end of the street and disappeared.

Blood pooled under the two dead men and flies landed on the open wounds and pieces of flesh. A woman screamed. Another fainted.

And looking down from above through an open window, Delbert Coombs muttered an audible curse that blasphemed God, Jesus, and his mother Mary.

The anger flared up through him and painted his face a ripe purple. He was soaking wet, but the water dried on his body just from the boiling heat of his skin.

"Blood for blood," he said to himself as he left the window and headed for the closet.

The sound of that rattle still echoed in his mind.

"Sidewinder, is he? Well, when I get through with him, he's going to be a dead sidewinder."

THIRTY-TWO

⚭

There were three cots in the small room where Felicity and Pilar were held prisoner.

The door was locked, as Maude said it would be, and all afternoon the two women had been listening to the voices downstairs, unable to understand what the people below were saying. But as the day wore on, Felicity began planning how they might escape. There was a single small window letting light into the room. But it was at the top of the wall, near the roof, and slatted to let air in.

Felicity looked at the bunks. They were made of lumber. Old, dirty mattresses and soiled blankets lay atop them under filthy pillows, one with the stuffing leaking out, old yellowed chicken feathers, and probably, she thought, families of lice.

Pilar had sat on the edge of a bunk and wept most of the afternoon. Quietly, Felicity thought, but she knew how the woman felt. She had tried to comfort Pilar, but the woman was distant and beyond any help that words or a touch could bring.

She walked over and knelt down in front of Pilar. She

reached up and smoothed the hair on the top of Pilar's head with her hand.

"Pilar, listen to me. Please. Forget about yourself and Julio for a moment, and please listen."

"I—I can't," Pilar said.

Felicity grabbed Pilar's chin and tilted her head so that she could look into her eyes.

"We can't just sit here, Pilar. We have to do something."

"What can we do?" Pilar's voice was weak and shaky, but Felicity had her attention.

"You have to help me. And we have to be very quiet. I want to take apart one of these cots. We can use the legs for clubs. Do you understand?"

"Yes. I—I think so. What good would that do? They are too many. They have guns."

"You're right, Pilar. But look, at least one of them has to come up here and bring us food and water. Or take us downstairs. If Maude comes up, we can beat her with our clubs and take away her gun."

"They will hear. They will come and shoot us."

"We have to do it quick, and we have to hit Maude or that Phil or Hiram real hard. They probably won't send the old man up. We have to be ready when we hear that key in the lock. And we have to hit real hard. We have to hit hard enough to kill whoever comes up. Do you think you can do that? Do you think you can help me? It might be our only chance."

"I will try, Felicity."

"Now, help me take that other bunk apart. We might have to pull and kick, but we can do it."

The two women lifted one corner of the bunk to look at its leg. Felicity threw the mattress, blanket, and pillow under Pilar's bunk.

"You grab onto the top, Pilar, and I'll start jerking this leg back and forth to loosen it. Hold on real tight."

"Yes," Pilar said, and set herself. She held the corner while Felicity pushed and pulled on the leg. She could feel it loosen. She heard a nail screech, and the sound startled her.

"We must be quiet," she whispered to Pilar, and began jerking the leg back and forth, twisting it until it loosened enough that she could wrestle it from the bed itself. She made sure it didn't strike the floor. She set the leg on Pilar's bunk.

"Now, the other side," she said.

The task completed, they waited on either side of the door, both with a makeshift club in hand. They waited and listened.

Downstairs, it was quiet. Then they heard the clanking of pans and utensils in the kitchen. The front door opened and closed. Footsteps back and forth. The front door opened again and stayed open for five minutes. Then it closed.

Felicity looked up at the small window. The light outside was fading. The room grew very dim.

Night was coming on.

And still, nobody had come up the stairs to bring them water or food. They were both hungry and thirsty.

"When will they come?" Pilar whispered.

"Shhh. I don't know. Just wait. Move your fingers so they don't get stiff. Be ready."

"I am ready," Pilar said.

They both felt the chill in the room as the sun set and darkness spilled in the window. Neither woman could see the other.

All they could hear was the sound of their own breathing.

All they could feel was the chill and the fear that nestled in their stomachs like something cold and crawling, like something they could only see in nightmares.

And then, they heard footsteps. Coming up the stairs.

Man or woman?

Felicity didn't know.

Tap, tap, tap, tap. So slow. So steady. The closer, the louder, and the taps turned to stomp, stomp, stomp.

Felicity pressed her ear against the wall.

Maude or one of the men?

The wait was nerve-racking.

Clump, clump, clump.

The key rattled in the lock. Both women stood up, holding their cudgels high, ready to strike.

The key turned in the lock.

The sound struck terror in Felicity's heart.

She held her breath.

She waited for the door to open.

The wait was an eternity in a single trickle of sand through the hour glass. One tick of the clock. One breath away from life—or death.

THIRTY-THREE

✺

Abner Wicks was surprised to see Delbert Coombs waiting outside the jail for him when he was released on bond by one Walter Stoval, Justice of the Peace.

Ridley Smoot was also surprised to see Delbert, who was sitting on his horse, but had the reins of two other horses in his hands. Both the riderless horses were saddled.

"Looks like Del's got a bee in his bonnet, Ab," Ridley said.

"And, looks like we're both going somewhere. Damn. I was hoping to get back to the High Grade."

"You and me, too."

"Come on boys," Delbert said. "Shake a leg."

The two men walked up to Delbert, and he handed reins to both of them.

"Mount up," he said. "Ridley, you're coming with me. Abner, you sonofabitch, you're going back up to the Storm ranch and hunt down that Mex what got away. There's grub aplenty in your saddlebags. You got a six-gun and a rifle. I want that bastard dead, you hear?"

"I hear you, Del," Wicks said. "Hell, ain't I got time for a drink?"

"You're lucky I don't shoot you where you stand. You got a bedroll there. You hurry, you can make it up there by morning. Hunt the Mex down, shoot him dead. And bring me proof."

"Proof?"

"Yeah, cut off his head. I want to see his dead face, or I'll come huntin' you, Abner, sure as you're standing there."

"Shit," said Abner, and mounted up. He saw the anger in Delbert's face, and he wanted no part of it. He checked his rifle, patted his full saddlebags.

"Be seein' ya, Ridley," he said, as he rode off.

"Where we goin', boss?" Ridley asked.

"To Ma's place. We got a heap of unfinished business."

Ridley settled in the saddle.

"Oh, that Storm feller?"

"Him and a Mex. Them first, then their women. Ain't gonna be no eyes on me, Ridley."

"No, sir."

"You see Kathy?"

"She come with the money for Stoval, then went back to the bank. Said she'd meet you tonight at the hotel."

"She'll be real sad when I ain't there," Delbert said.

"Say, where is that Storm feller anyways? Him and that Mex."

"My guess is that they'll be at Ma's before us. I hope they're waitin', or else Ma and Pa have done put their lamps out."

"I guess we'll burn some gunpowder tonight, Del."

"You can bet on that, Ridley. I hold most of the good cards in this deck."

"You know what that Storm feller calls hisself?"

"I heard. Sidewinder."

"Funny moniker."

"Well, you know what they do to sidewinders out in Arizona, don't you?"

"No, sir, I reckon not."

"They shoot their heads plumb off, that's what they do, Ridley."

Ridley grinned.

"You gonna shoot Storm's head off?"

"Yeah, after I shoot off his balls."

Del put the spurs to his horse, and the two men galloped off. The sun was falling in the west, hanging there above the snowcapped peaks like a blazing golden cauldron, firing the clouds strung out across the sky like gilded coffins all lined up, waiting to be loaded on the night's caissons.

It was a glorious sunset, by any man's measure, and it was just starting, Ridley thought.

And there was blood in it, as well as gold.

THIRTY-FOUR

～

They hid their horses behind a hillock and walked a quarter of a mile to Pete's old observation post. By the time they reached the copse of trees, the sun had set and the light was fading in the glowing western sky. All three men carried their rifles. Brad and Julio had reloaded their six-guns as they left Oro City.

"You can see the layout," Pete said. "Mite near impregnable. I mean you can't ride across that bridge without coming under fire. Can you see the gunports?"

"Just barely," Brad said, but his mind was already working, and he saw a way in. He would have the darkness, too.

"I'm going to make a wide loop," he said, "and come in from the right. You two stay here with your rifles. I'll leave mine here, so you'll have one extra."

"There are gunports on the sides of the house, too," Pete said.

"I'm going to crawl to the front door. Under the front gunports. I doubt if they'll have rifles poking out those side ones."

"Maybe."

He handed his rifle to Julio, took off his hat.

"You watch that front door. If it opens and somebody steps outside and it's one of them, shoot."

"Then, what will you do?" Pete asked.

Brad was already hunched over, walking to the south of their position.

"I'm going in with my six-gun blazing," he said.

The dark came on fast. Brad waded across the creek about a hundred yards from the house. He took it slow, so he wouldn't splash. When he got directly opposite the front of the house, he dropped to his belly and began to crawl.

He pushed one knee forward, then brought up the other a foot or so at a time. He crawled over grass, cactus, and rocks, and around brush. When he got to the side, he raised his head and looked up. No rifles in the side gunports.

He crawled on.

When he reached the front door, he saw a rifle barrel poking through a gunport on that side. The windows were all shuttered, but he could see a thin rim of light as someone inside lit a lamp.

He stood up and flattened himself against the house, held his breath.

Then he took out his rattle and held it right next to the gunport. He shook it furiously, and the rattling made his skin jump. He heard a commotion inside.

"They's a damn rattlesnake a-tryin' to get in the house." A man's voice, yelling.

The front door opened, and Brad shook the rattle faster.

The old man stepped out, a rifle in his hand.

There was the crack of a rifle from across the creek and road.

The old man clutched his chest and staggered for two or three steps, then pitched forward. He hit the ground with a thud.

Brad crouched and ran through the door. The man at the gunport to his right turned and stared at him. He was young and big. He started to pull the rifle from the gunport when Brad shot him, right between the eyes.

The man tumbled backward and collapsed in a grotesque sprawl, blood oozing from a black hole between his eyebrows. His straw hair was stippled with blood drops as if he had been looking into an exploding can of barn paint.

There was shouting and screaming from upstairs. A man entered the front room, a tray of food in his hand.

"Hey," he yelled, and dropped the tray. Food splattered everywhere as he bent down into a fighting crouch, and his hand flew to the pistol on his hip.

Brad shook the rattle with his left hand.

The man lost that one second of time.

Brad squeezed the trigger and his .44 Colt exploded, spewing lead and orange sparks, smoke and flame from the muzzle.

"You . . . you . . ."

The bullet struck the man in the throat and ripped it out in a spray of bright red blood. He gurgled and fell to his knees, clawing at his throat, struggling to pull in air.

His throat went into convulsions, and Brad heard his death rattle as he raced past him and took the stairs two at a time.

Women were screaming, and he heard the thud of blows.

He ran down the dark hall to an open door where the screams were loudest.

He stood there, trying to see into the room. Someone lay on the floor. He saw a woman's legs and shoes.

"Felicity?" Brad said, and stepped to one side of the door, outside, in the hall.

"Brad," she screamed. "Help us."

Then he heard Pilar babbling in Spanish.

"She is dead," Pilar screamed. "You killed her."

Brad stepped inside the room, dreading what he might see.

THIRTY-FIVE

❧

Less than a mile from his mother's home, Delbert and Ridley heard gunfire. Both men stopped their horses to listen.

Then it was quiet.

"I counted three shots," Ridley said.

"Maybe it's all over," Delbert said. "You ride up and see what's been going on, Ridley. I'll be right behind you."

"Why me, Del?"

"Don't argue with me. Take it slow. Likely, you'll see the Mex and Storm lying dead right out front. Now get moving."

Julio and Pete were waiting for Ridley when he rode up. They pointed their rifles at him from twenty feet away.

"Off your horse, Smoot," Pete said.

"I'm damned," Ridley said, seeing that he had no chance to retreat. As he was climbing down from the saddle, Pete and Julio braced him from two sides. He stared at rifle barrels less than a foot from his face.

The three men heard a flurry of hoofbeats heading toward town.

"That Delbert?" Pete asked, lifting Ridley's pistol from its holster.

"That bastard," Ridley said.

~

"Is she dead?" Felicity asked as Brad stepped over Maude's body. Felicity's voice was quavering, and she still held the makeshift club in her hand.

Pilar was pressed against Felicity's back, trembling, sobbing.

"Yes," Brad said, and took the board from Felicity's hand and dropped it on the floor. "Let's go. Pilar, Julio's outside, waiting for you."

~

Julio set down his rifle and took Pilar in his arms. They spoke to each other in Spanish.

"Looks like you'll be working for Harry, Brad," Pete said. "Delbert Coombs hightailed it after throwing Smoot here to the dogs. Julio and I were the dogs."

"If it means bringing Coombs to justice, then I'm in Harry's employ."

Pete looked at Smoot.

"You're going to hang, Ridley. All by yourself, I guess."

Ridley looked at Brad, a wry smile on his face. He saw the rattles hanging from Brad's neck.

"I heard about those rattles," he said. "Wicks told me you scared hell out of him."

"Where is Wicks?" Brad asked.

"He's on his way up to your ranch. He'll be there by tomorrow. Del sent him to kill that other Mex, the one you left behind."

Julio and Brad exchanged looks.

"Don't be too sure about that, Smoot," Brad said.

~

Abner Wicks circled the desolated remains of the Storm ranch. He saw no sign of the Mexican. He could still smell the acrid odor of the fire. The scent stung his nostrils. He was about to turn his horse and ride back to Oro City when he saw movement from the trees above the burned barn.

Carlos rose up from his hiding place, a Winchester rifle at his shoulder.

Wicks reached for his own rifle.

That was the last act of his life.

Carlos squeezed the trigger. The bullet fried the air with sizzling speed and struck Abner Wicks just to the right of his breastbone. His heart exploded inside his shattered rib cage.

He fell to the ground, dead.

And now, Carlos thought, I have a horse.

Now, while there was still daylight, he would ride into Oro City to find Brad and Julio.

He looked down at the body of Abner Wicks as he grabbed up his horse's reins.

"And, you," he said, "will be food for the wolves and the buzzards."

~

Harry Pendergast handed Brad a thick envelope as Pete and Felicity looked on.

"What's this?" Brad said.

"Salary and expenses, Brad. And, your first assignment."

"I have an assignment already?"

Pendergast smiled.

"I expect Delbert Coombs might lead you a merry chase. He'll show up somewhere. His kind always do. I want him brought to justice. You know what justice is, don't you?"

Brad smiled.

"Yes, I know what justice is. I have revised that old Mexican saying."

"Oh?"

"Yes. Now, it's 'There is justice in the world.'"

He put his arm around Felicity and squeezed her tight against him.

Then he handed her the sealed envelope, reached into his pocket, pulled out a wad of greenbacks, and handed those to her, as well.

"What's this for?" she asked.

"A new life," Brad said. "A new home."

"Welcome to the Denver Detective Agency," Pendergast said, handing Felicity a hotel key. "You'll stay in the Clarendon's honeymoon suite until you find a place of your own," he said.

Felicity felt her knees go weak. She felt faint until Brad kissed her, breathing new life into her heart and soul.

"Let's see if that key works," he whispered.

PETER BRANDVOLD

DEALT THE DEVIL'S HAND

With a bloodthirsty posse prepared to pump him full of hot lead, bounty hunter Lou Prophet tries to steer clear of the sweet young thing who's making him think twice about his drifter lifestyle.

THE DEVIL AND LOU PROPHET

Call him manhunter, tracker, or bounty hunter. Lou Prophet loved his work—it kept him in wine and women, and was never dull. His latest job sounds particularly attractive: he's to escort to the courthouse a showgirl who's a prime witness in a murder trial. But some very dangerous men are moving in to make sure the pair never reach the courthouse alive.

M33AS0907